TWO TALES BY
CHARLOTTE BRONTË
"THE SECRET" &
"LILY HART"

TRANSCRIBED FROM THE ORIGINAL
MANUSCRIPT AND EDITED BY
WILLIAM HOLTZ

UNIVERSITY OF MISSOURI PRESS

COLUMBIA & LONDON

1978

Illustrations

Grateful acknowledgment is given to The Brontë Society, Haworth, for granting permission to use the illustrations shown on the following pages: pp. 1, 6, 8, 12, 14, 31, 32

Copyright © 1978 by The Curators of the University of Missouri
University of Missouri Press, Columbia, Missouri 65201
Library of Congress Catalog Card Number 77-11182
Printed and bound in the United States of America

Library of Congress Cataloging in Publication Data

Brontë, Charlotte, 1816–1855.
    Two Tales by Charlotte Brontë.

    CONTENTS: The Secret.—Lily Hart.
    1. Brontë, Charlotte, 1816–1855—Manuscripts—Facsimiles.
I. Holtz, William V.   II. Title: Brontë, Charlotte, 1816–1855.
Lily Hart. 1978.
PZ3.B790Ty 1978 [PR4166]   823'.8   77–11182
ISBN, cloth edition, 0–8262–0232–2;
slipcase numbered edition, 0–8262–0245–4

FOR VICTORIA
FROM HER FATHER
IN HONOR OF HER
TWENTY-FIRST YEAR

Acknowledgments   I would like to thank the following people for their help at various stages in the preparation of this book. My major obligation is to James W. Symington, whose gift of the Brontë manuscript to the University of Missouri made this undertaking possible. I am indebted to several of my colleagues in the Department of English for their aid and advice: Professors Donald Anderson, Lloyd Berry, J. Donald Crowley, Milton M. Gatch, William Peden, and John R. Roberts. Professor Emerita Mildred Christian of Tulane University and Anthony Garnett were helpful in regard to certain features of the manuscript. Dwight Tuckwood and Margaret Howell of the library staff were trustworthy guardians of the manuscript. Rose McClure, Margaret Butler, and Marjorie Wallace offered me skilled secretarial help when I needed it. Corinne Davis cheerfully typed the difficult final manuscript. Finally, I must mention the many times my wife, Lora, willingly put aside her own work to help me with mine: every page here bears her impress.

I was also materially aided by the Research Council of the University of Missouri–Columbia, who granted me a Summer Research Fellowship for the initial stages of this work and who provided funds for the final preparation of the manuscript.

...ther — Painted by Martin
...ed by B. B. — Bronte Decr. 1830

Preface   This book is an edition of and a commentary on a tiny manuscript containing "The Secret" and "Lily Hart," two stories that are part of Charlotte Brontë's juvenilia. The manuscript was found among the possessions of Mrs. Evelyn Symington, wife of U.S. Senator Stuart M. Symington, after her death in 1973. It was presented to the University of Missouri in 1975 by U.S. Congressman James W. Symington.

A Note on the Text.   The Brontë juvenilia are characterized by their minute size and almost microscopic handwriting. This particular manuscript consists of no more than four sheets of notepaper folded into a sixteen-page book of $4\frac{1}{2}$ inches long and $3\frac{5}{8}$ inches wide[1] and contains approximately nineteen thousand words. On the title page, Charlotte inscribed the pseudonym "Charles Wellesley," the name she often used in the other juvenilia. "The Secret" begins on page 3 of the manuscript, and "Lily Hart" begins midway through page 11. The last page of text (page 15 of the manuscript) is signed "Charlotte Brontë" and dated "November 7ᵗʰ, —33." She was then seventeen years old.

The reader who turns to the accompanying facsimile will see the problems of editing the Brontë juvenilia. Not only is the script almost microscopic, but the punctuation is rudimentary, often inconsistent, and frequently simply absent. With these difficulties in mind, I have attempted in this edition to serve two readers, not only the accomplished Brontë specialist but also what Samuel Johnson approvingly called "the common reader." For the second I have provided an edited text, supplying punctuation and

---

1. The manuscript, now in the rare book collection of the Elmer Ellis Library, University of Missouri–Columbia, has been cut apart where the notepaper was originally folded, so it appears to be made of eight sheets. Technically, it originally could have been folded and cut from one sheet.

paragraph divisions and normalizing spelling and capitalization to conform to modern British usage. Where the text is obscure, I have indicated my suggested reading with square brackets. Wholly illegible words or passages are similarly indicated. Of course, such editorial normalizing does destroy the unique effect of the tiny manuscript and the sense of feverishly intense composition that its text suggests; thus I have included a facsimile of the manuscript in its entirety. Finally, I have provided introductory material and appendixes that will permit an informed appreciation of these tales in their larger context. The Brontë scholar will have less need for these aids, but he will perhaps find useful the photographic enlargements of the manuscript and my attempt to transcribe the original as accurately as the difficulties of the manuscript allow.

Provenance of the Manuscript.   Apparently the first person outside the Brontë family to see this manuscript—or any of the Brontë juvenilia—was Elizabeth Gaskell, who, while gathering material for a biography just after Charlotte's death, visited the Reverend Patrick Brontë, Charlotte's father, and examined some of these early works. She chose to reproduce the first page of "The Secret" to illustrate this phase of Charlotte's work.[2] Since Gaskell's publication of Charlotte's *Life* in 1857, this page has been all that has been known of the manuscript. Presumably it traveled to Ireland with Charlotte's husband, the Reverend Arthur Bell Nicholls, and returned to England among the trove of juvenilia purchased from Nicholls by Clement Shorter in 1895, which passed to T. J. Wise.[3] At this point it probably received its present leather

---

2. Elizabeth Gaskell, *The Life of Charlotte Brontë*, 2 vols. (London, 1857), 1:84.

3. Clement Shorter, *The Brontës: Life and Letters*, 2 vols. (London, 1908; reprinted New York, 1969), 1:19–20; T. J. Wise and J. A. Symington, eds.,

binding, as Wise dispersed many of the individual manuscripts on the marketplace as literary curiosities. This provenance is conjectural, however; the only recorded appearances since the Gaskell biography are Shorter's listing [4] and a note of its sale in New York in 1915.[5] At some time after this date it came into the possession of Mrs. Symington.

The appropriate place for insertion of these tales into the Brontë canon has for a long time been marked. Half a century after Gaskell gave the world notice of the juvenile writings and reproduced a single page, Shorter prepared a chronology of the works that had come to his hand;[6] and with the publication of the Shakespeare Head edition of the Brontës' *Works*, the position of these two tales in the sequence of Charlotte's early writing was prepared in the hope that they would eventually be recovered.[7] Like minor stars plucked out from a constellation, their loss diminished but did not obscure our knowledge of the elaborate epic narrative that claimed Charlotte's imagination in her youth. Now, after more than one hundred twenty years, the first of the juvenilia to reach the public eye becomes the latest to be incorporated into our knowledge of Charlotte Brontë's work.

The Miscellaneous and Unpublished Writings of Charlotte and Patrick Branwell Brontë, vols. 8 and 9 of the Shakespeare Head edition of the Brontës' works (London, 1936–1938), 9:471–73. J. A. Symington is no relative of the American Symington family who later owned the manuscript.

4. Shorter, 2:431.

5. Mildred G. Christian, "A Census of Brontë Manuscripts in the United States," *The Trollopian* 2 (1947–1948):190. The prefatory material to this list also describes T. J. Wise's irresponsible handling of the manuscripts.

6. Shorter, 2:430–34.

7. Wise and Symington, 8:314.

CONTENTS

Alexander Percy Esq.re M.P.
Ætat 21.

THE SECRET

AND

[handwritten, largely illegible cursive]

THE SECRET

CHAPTER THE 1st

A dead silence had reigned in the Home office of Vespopolis for three hours on the morning of a fine summer's day interrupted only by such sounds as the scraping of a penknife, the dropping of water, an occasional cough or whisper, & now & then some brief immediate uttered by the whole Secretary in his communicating tones: at length that sublime personage, after completing some report to its despatches, addressing a small sub... with young gentlemen who occupied the chief situations around the clerk's, he said "M.r Rymer will you be good enough to tell me what o'clock it is" "Certainly my lord" said the speaker...

[remainder of page illegible handwritten manuscript]

CHAPTER THE IInd

All the glory of
~~Soon~~ I look will see
While sunshine ~~so~~ so mournfully
Through the blue gleaming

O these deep hollow tones
Sad thoughts inspire
They ~~would~~ like the thrilling ~~notes~~
Before ~~the~~ swept lyre

Echoes from rock & cave
Silently lying
Answer the howling wave
Track the winds sighing

Far in the silent sky
wandering worlds ~~grieve~~
Thus they shall beam on high
Conquest for ever

But we neither ~~mourn~~
Silvery like willow
Ocean will be my tomb
Sea-sand my pillow

Then my unhallowed name
None shall remember
Gone like the living flame
Quenched like the ember

CHAPTER THE III.

CHAPTER THE IV.th

LILY HART

Dark is the mansion of the dead
  Dark desolate and still
Around it broods a solemn dread
  Within a cheerless chill

O mother! does thy spirit rest
  In fairer worlds than ours?
And ever slumber hours?

I trust it doth for thy pale clay
  Hath found me fast asleep
Sweet ... the happy light of day
  Pressed by the cold ... bed

Yet mother I would rest with thee
  In ... dreamless sleep
Though fixed its mute solemnity
  All voiceless, still & deep

And I would rest my weary head
  Upon thy lifeless breast
Nor feel ... shuddering thrill of dread
  At what my ... priest

Heaven is a dreary void to me
  Heaven is a cloud of gloom
Safe in thy stilly ... sleep with the

General
Introduction

The imagination enlarges little objects so
as to fill our souls with a fantastic
estimate.—Pascal, *Penseé*, 84

The way to an understanding of the tales in this manuscript is made
easier by a preliminary glimpse into one of the most fascinating childhood
enterprises recorded in our literature. The place to begin is with the impact
upon the receptive imaginations of four talented children of a simple gift—
a set of twelve wooden soldiers. The gift was for the only boy, Patrick
Branwell Brontë; but he shared the toys with Charlotte, Emily, and Anne,
each of whom claimed and named one soldier as a special hero.[1] These
figures, thus born into fictive existence, were nourished in an atmosphere
rich in literary, artistic, and political interests: the children read avidly in
Blackwood's Magazine, the weekly press, and their father's library; and the
father, himself the author of five volumes, treated his children as equals in
wide-ranging discussions of contemporary affairs. The immediate result of
the arrival of the soldiers was the establishment of a series of "plays," as
Charlotte called them: interconnected stories of the Twelve Adventurers,
their founding of a kingdom in Africa, and the subsequent exploits of their
descendants and the followers that soon populated the various provinces of
this imaginary land.

Our attention must focus on Charlotte and, to a lesser extent, on Branwell; for in time Emily and Anne withdrew from the original enterprise to
develop a separate mythical kingdom. Charlotte and Branwell, however,
continued to elaborate the narrative of The Twelves, as the heroes came to
be called, in a series of miniature hand-printed books, presumably propor-
tioned to the size of the original toy figures. Charlotte's chosen soldier had
been named after the Duke of Wellington, reflecting her enthusiasm for
England's national hero. He was soon established as the ruler of his own
African kingdom; others of the heroes were assigned their kingdoms in a
loose confederation centering in The Great Glass Town, later called
Verdopolis. "The dark hinterland of the novels," an artistic and moral
"chaos," Kathleen Tillotson has called these uniquely cooperative, invo-
luted, and self-referential early tales by Charlotte and Branwell:

> Since [the tales] themselves issued from a corporate daydream,
> nothing ever needed to be explained; each piece assumed a knowledge

---

1. Elizabeth Gaskell, *The Life of Charlotte Brontë*, 2 vols. (London, 1857), 1:89.

not only of all the rest but of much that was "made out" only in talk or solitary imaginings. As the amorphous mass swelled and sprawled, it became impossible to envisage "outside" readers; the large problems of structure, the delicate question of guiding the interest—in a word, of communication—were never faced. There is no Angrian story that can be read with the serene confidence that, whatever happens, the writer is in control.[2]

The control, artistic and moral, Charlotte would achieve; but only by way of outgrowing Branwell and the Angrian tales into a disciplined life of writing. At this early stage, however, her brother's mark lies heavily upon Charlotte's work: both of the stories here presented assume a background of his creation.

This background was largely a realm of military adventure and political intrigue. Charlotte's imagination, however, turned to the themes of passion and suffering, which she explored mainly through the career of a second-generation hero, Arthur Augustus Adrian Wellesley, Marquis of Douro and later Duke of Zamorna and Emperor of Angria. Douro, as she called him in the earlier tales, grew largely out of her adolescent reading of Byron: nobly handsome, fatally attractive to almost every woman, Douro united in one frame all the talents of poet, warrior, and statesman. From her thirteenth to her twenty-third years, Charlotte chronicled his many loves and political vicissitudes; eventually he re-emerges as the Rochester of *Jane Eyre*. Perhaps as a defense against uncritical indulgence, she chose to write of her hero from the point of view of his critical, envious younger brother, Lord Charles Wellesley. Lord Charles (whose name echoes Charlotte's) is the narrator of both tales here presented. Douro's personal life provides the subject of "The Secret," while "Lily Hart" involves peripheral figures caught up in the civil disorder at which Douro is the center.

These tales come approximately midway in Charlotte's elaboration of the Glass Town epic. In this larger context, it is the precocity and persistence of the impulse to write that is more impressive than any individual performance; and these two tales do betray the inevitable awkwardness of a juvenile writer, particularly in their huddled conclusions. Indeed, the whole Brontë juvenile canon raises very clearly the problem of the "value"

---

2. Kathleen Tillotson, *Novels of the Eighteen-Forties* (Oxford, 1954), pp. 270–71.

of the immature work of writers who achieve mature masterpieces. The appropriate question, of course, is that of genesis, not only of imaginative power but of theme and technique to embody that power. Little I might say in this regard would add to what Fannie Ratchford has bequeathed to Brontë scholars in her landmark study of the juvenilia.[3] For the more casual reader, however, who has perhaps felt the force of *Jane Eyre* and who may smile indulgently at these slight but charming tales, I would offer some hint of the creative energy seeking expression at this early stage.

The most curious evidence, perhaps, comes in one of the earliest of the tales, written when Charlotte was fourteen. Her narrator, Lord Charles, finds himself caught up mysteriously in an intersection of his world and the supervening order of his creator, as Charlotte dramatizes the power of the creative imagination:

> It seemed as if I was a non-existent shadow—that I neither spoke, eat [*sic*], imagined, or lived of myself, but I was the mere idea of some other creature's brain. The Glass Town seemed so likewise. My father, Arthur, and everyone with whom I am acquainted, passed into a state of annihilation. . . . at the end of a long vista, as it were, appeared dimly and indistinctly, beings that really lived in a tangible shape, that were called by our names and were US from whom WE had been copied by something—I could not tell what.
>
> . . . I was roused by a loud noise above my head. I looked up and thick obscurity was before my eyes. Voices—one like my own but larger and dimmer (if sound may be characterised by such epithets) and another, which sounded familiar, yet I had never that I could remember heard it before—murmuring unceasingly in my ears.
>
> I saw books removing from the top shelves and returning, apparently of their own accord. By degrees the mistiness cleared off. I felt myself raised suddenly to the ceiling, and ere I was aware, behold two immense sparkling bright blue globes within a few yards of me. I was in a hand wide enough almost to grasp the Tower of all Nations, and when it lowered me to the floor I saw a huge personification of myself—hundreds of feet high—standing against the great Oriel.
>
> This filled me with a weight of astonishment greater than the mind

---

3. Fannie Ratchford, *The Brontës' Web of Childhood* (New York, 1941). With every other student of Brontë juvenilia, I am fundamentally indebted to this work.

of man ever before had to endure, and I was now perfectly convinced of my non-existence except in another corporeal frame which dwelt in the real world, for ours I thought was nothing but idea.[4]

More direct testimony appears later, when Charlotte writes in her own person of the intensity of her commitment to the creatures of her imagination:

> I hear them speak . . . I see distinctly their figures—and though alone, I experience all the feelings of one admitted for the first time into a grand circle of classic beings—recognising by tone, gesture and aspect hundreds whom I never saw before, but whom I have heard of many a time, and is not this enjoyment? . . . There is one just now crossing—a lady I will not write her name though I know it—no history is connected with her identity, she is not one of the transcendantly [sic] fair and inaccessible sacred beings—whose fates are interwoven with the highest of the high— I cannot write of them except in total solitude I scarce dare think of them.[5]

As we contemplate, then, the achieved power of *Jane Eyre* and *Villette*, we must recognize that they did not spring unprecedented from a mind turned late to fiction. Rather, they are the culmination of a passionate life of writing. The early efforts, such as the tales here presented, are diminutive and crudely drawn; but they tap the impulse of genius and cast long shadows forward toward her mature work. The way to that work was to be by arduous renunciation, as she reluctantly turned from indulgence in dream and fantasy to the discipline of the realistic novel. The transition took place gradually: as early as 1839, she rehearsed in a fragmentary passage the leave-taking that would be complete by 1846, the date of her first-written but last-published novel, *The Professor*. The earlier manuscript records the crucial change of mood with regret:

> I have now written a great many books and for a long time have dwelt on the same characters and scenes and subjects. . . . but we must change,

---

4. "Strange Events," *The Young Men's Magazine* (December 1830), in *The Miscellaneous and Unpublished Writings of Charlotte and Patrick Branwell Brontë*, ed. T. J. Wise and J. A. Symington (London, 1936–1938), 8:19–20.

5. "Roe Head Journal" (1836). Quoted from Winifred Gérin, *Charlotte Brontë: The Evolution of Genius* (Oxford, 1967), p. 106. This collection of fragmentary jottings shows clearly how Charlotte was literally possessed by the creatures of her imagination.

for the eye is tired of the picture so oft recurring and now so familiar.

Yet do not urge me too fast, reader: it is no easy theme to dismiss from my imagination the images which have filled it so long; they were my friends and my intimate acquaintances. . . . Still, I long to quit for awhile that burning clime where we have sojourned too long—its skies aflame— the glow of sunset is always upon it—the mind would cease from excitement and turn now to a cooler region where the dawn breaks grey and sober, and the coming day for a time at least is subdued by clouds.[6]

By the time of *The Professor*, the scrupulous damping of her fancy produced a work so austere that it would be published only after her death, when her renown would assure an audience that the novel alone could not have gained earlier. The preface, written in retrospect after she had attained fame, gives us some notion of the strictures she had placed on herself:

I had got over any such taste as I might once have had for ornamented and redundant composition, and come to prefer what was plain and homely. . . .

I said to myself that my hero should work his way through life as I had seen real living men work theirs—that he should never get a shilling he had not earned—that no sudden turns should lift him in a moment to wealth and high station; that whatever small competency he might gain, should be won by the sweat of his brow; that, before he could find so much as an arbour to sit down in, he should master at least half the ascent of "the Hill of Difficulty;" that he should not even marry a beautiful girl or a lady of rank. As Adam's son he should share Adam's doom, and drain throughout life a mixed and moderate cup of enjoyment.[7]

Such extreme restraint, however, was not her natural mode, as every reader of *Jane Eyre* will recognize; and even *Villette*, a reworking of much of the material of *The Professor*, is in fact an accommodation of this program to her earlier mode—clumsily, in the Gothic claptrap of the ghostly nun, artfully in the prolonged analysis of Lucy Snowe's emotional trauma. The two tales that follow will give a fair representation of the "burning clime" of her early years that would be naturalized and rationalized—but never wholly denied—in her mature fiction.

A more detailed account of the Brontë juvenilia would be dispropor-

---

6. "The Last of Angria," Wise and Symington, 9:403–4.
7. Quoted here from the Shakespeare Head edition.

The Great Glasstown Confederacy, from a drawing by Branwell Brontë.

tionate here; but the reader interested in further exploration can begin with Fannie Ratchford's painstaking reconstruction of the saga in *The Brontës' Web of Childhood* (New York, 1941), based on her study of most of the surviving manuscripts—approximately one hundred forty in all. Many of these are transcribed in volumes 8–9 of the Shakespeare Head edition of the Brontës' *Works*, edited by T. J. Wise and J. A. Symington. Selected tales are printed in *Legends of Angria*, edited by Fannie Ratchford and William Clyde DeVane (New Haven, 1933); *The Twelve Adventurers and Other Stories*, edited by C. W. Hatfield (London, 1925); *Tales from Angria*, edited by Phillis Bentley (London, 1954); and *Five Novelettes*, edited by Winifred Gérin (London, 1971). Individual tales published separately include *The Spell: An Extravaganza*, edited by G. E. McLean (London, 1931); "A Leaf from an Unopened Volume," edited by A. Edward Newton in his *Derby Day and Other Adventures* (Boston, 1934); "An Interesting Passage," edited by Judith Chernaik, *London Times Literary Supplement* (23 November 1973); and "The Search After Hapiness [sic]," edited by T. A. J. Burnett (London and New York, 1969).

Introduction
"The Secret"
The focus in "The Secret" falls not upon Charlotte's major hero, Douro, but upon his delicate child bride Marian Hume and his archrival Sir Alexander Percy. Marian is presented to us at approximately the midpoint of her brief marriage to Douro. Earlier Charlotte had recorded their idyllic courtship and betrothal; later Marian is supplanted in Douro's affections by the more assertively passionate Mary Percy, daughter of Alexander Percy by an earlier marriage than the one here described. In this tale, Percy's second marriage, to Zenobia Ellrington, has elevated him from a mere adventurer to the nobility; for Zenobia, it is a painful bondage, exacerbated by the fact that earlier she had been Marian's rival for Douro's love. But her sterner character serves her better than Marian's pliant nature: she survives, even as Douro's affections turn to her step-daughter, while the abandoned Marian dies of grief, attended by the noble John of Fidena.[1]

Percy we encounter here shortly after his metamorphosis in Charlotte's imagination from the pirate Alexander Rogue introduced into the tales by Branwell. Throughout the subsequent narratives he remains Douro's major antagonist: a brilliant, dissolute, unprincipled demagogue, at one point leading a civil insurrection and at another striking an uneasy alliance as premier in Douro's new kingdom of Angria.[2] The relationship is one of

---

1. This tangle of relationships emerges from "Albion and Marina" (1830), "The Bridal" (1832), "A Peep into a Picture Book" (1834), in *The Miscellaneous and Unpublished Writings of Charlotte and Patrick Branwell Brontë*, ed. T. J. Wise and J. A. Symington (London, 1936–1938), 8:24, 202, 358–60 (these tales by Charlotte); and from "The Pirate" (1833), Wise and Symington, 8:170 (by Branwell). See also Fannie Ratchford, *The Brontës' Web of Childhood* (New York, 1941), summary, pp. 73–76.

2. He is the revolutionary leader executed at the end of the civil war described in Branwell's "Letters from an Englishman," (1830–1832), Wise and Symington, 8:96 (see Appendix II). Resurrected, he is given an earlier history by Charlotte in "The Green Dwarf" (1833), conveniently readable in Fannie Ratchford and William Clyde DeVane, *Legends of Angria* (New Haven, 1933), pp. 1–102. As Douro's premier he ultimately engages in a conspiracy that sends Douro temporarily into exile. Upon Douro's regaining ascendancy, he and Percy reach an uneasy truce, the last complication being Douro's affair with Percy's nubile daughter, Caroline Vernon. Part of this series of events is Branwell's, part Charlotte's: for a convenient summary, see Ratchford, *Web of Childhood*, pp. 99–132. Significant continuous portions are in Charlotte's "Zamorna's Exile" and "Caroline Vernon," available in

mutual enmity and fascination; between them, Percy and Douro mark the poles of Charlotte's adolescent conception of masculine grandeur.

The opening vignette has very little to do with the story that follows, but it does illustrate how seamless was Charlotte's conception of the affairs of this imaginary realm. For Edward and Julia Sydney flow into these opening pages from her earlier tale "The Foundling," although they are here reduced from romantic lovers to figures of domestic comedy.[3] This tonal shift is itself a pattern internal to the tale Charlotte's narrator tells in "The Secret," for the detached, ironic voice of Lord Charles is only intermittently dominant, emerging again from the rhapsodic flow of the narrative only to observe Douro at breakfast, Alexander Percy and Zenobia in their domestic discourse, or, more faintly, to record the mildly farcical conclusion of the melodrama. This oscillation is frequent in the juvenile tales and would seem to reflect an attempt to gain a controlled perspective on powerfully emotional materials. The framing of romantic love against a background of blackmail, bigamy, and deceit prefigures *Jane Eyre* in several ways, as do the evocation of atmosphere and setting, the suggestion of fairy tale, and the intrusion of the supernatural. Only with the creation of Jane herself, however, would Charlotte find a narrator capable at once of responding wholly to the potential of such material and subordinating it to the discipline of a mature and occasionally sardonic intelligence.

Here, however, in the early stages of the Angrian cycle, Charlotte's developing inventive faculty strains to lay the most excruciating tortures upon her most pathetic heroine: what worse for poor Marian, whose only strength is her love for Douro, than to discover in the early years of her marriage that she is still bound by a childhood betrothal to a man long thought dead? and that her natural father is not Alexander Hume but Alexander Percy, a vicious degenerate and her husband's bitterest enemy? It is an elaborate hoax, we find, but Charlotte uses it to dabble with themes of incest and bigamy. Out of such melodramatic materials comes the most extended portrait of Charlotte's first heroine, who is soon to disappear, however, as Charlotte seeks less innocent, more complexly motivated women to set over against Douro's erotic energy. Mary Percy, Alexander's daughter, will succeed her in Douro's affections: Marian can only languish

---

Ratchford, *Legends of Angria*. "Caroline Vernon" has been re-edited and published in a more complete form by Winifred Gérin, *Five Novelettes* (London, 1971).

3. Wise and Symington, 8:220.

and die, but in Mary's future lie Douro's liaisons with Mina Laury and Caroline Vernon, which will evoke in her resolute stratagems to claim her due.[4] Mina Laury, we might observe in passing, stands in this story in much the same inferior relation to Douro as will Jane Eyre to Rochester. In later narratives, Mina develops into Douro's devoted mistress: resilient, capable, utterly selfless, she is at his side in another period of civil strife and during his subsequent exile.

The brothers Percy who appear here are among the several sons of Alexander who figure in the Angrian cycle. All apparently suffer from their father's unnatural hatred and persecution. In various combinations they afford Charlotte opportunity to develop themes through contrasting pairs; the brothers Crimsworth of *The Professor* are recognizable descendants of this early family, the mercenary Edward of this story evolving into a grasping merchant in Verdopolis and finally into Edward Crimsworth.[5] Henry Percy, however, until the discovery of this tale, had been known only through Charlotte's "Stanzas on the Fate of Henry Percy" (1834).[6] As Fannie Ratchford noted, this poem posed a curious problem in the Angrian cycle, for it came after the death of Marian Hume but recorded her childhood betrothal to Henry Percy—her posthumous husband, Ratchford termed him.[7] Now, however, we can see that Charlotte's conception was not so laxly organized; for the early marriage had emerged in "The Secret" prior to the poem, as Charlotte sought narrative situations to test her radically simple heroine. The "Stanzas" then mark a return to "The Secret"; Charlotte re-creates in the poem Marian's painful transition from childish to adult love as perceived by Percy in his dreams aboard ship in the South Seas. Poem complements tale point for point, as the later work verifies the death (at his father's command) that Henry's ghost had attested in "The Secret."

---

4. "Passing Events" and "Caroline Vernon," ed. Gérin, *Five Novelettes.*

5. This sequence is traced nicely by Ratchford, *Web of Childhood*, pp. 190–200. Edward Percy later marries Maria Sneaky, who appears in the opening pages of this story—and who is sister to John of Fidena of "Lily Hart."

6. See Appendix I for the text of this poem.

7. Ratchford, *Web of Childhood*, p. 88. At about the same time, Charlotte creates a parallel adolescent marriage for Douro—to Helen Victorina, who dies in childbirth (Ratchford, *Web of Childhood*, p. 85).

THE SECRET

CHAPTER THE 1st

A dead silence had reigned in the Home Office of Verdopolis for three hours on the morning of a fine summer's day, interrupted only by such sounds as the scraping of a penknife, the dropping of a ruler, an occasional cough or whisper, and now and then some brief mandate, uttered by the noble first secretary, in his commanding tones. At length that sublime personage, after completing some score or so of despatches, addressing a small, slightly built young gentleman who occupied the chief situation among the clerks, said:

'Mr. Rhymer, will you be good enough to tell me what o'clock it is?'

'Certainly, my lord!' was the prompt reply as, springing from his seat, the ready underling, instead of consulting his watch like other people, hastened to the window in order to mark the sun's situation; having made his observations, he answered:

''Tis twelve precisely, my lord.'

'Very well', said the marquis. 'You may all give up then, and see that your desks are locked, and that not a scrap of paper is left to litter the office. Mr. Rhymer, I shall expect you to take care that my directions are fulfilled.' So saying, he assumed his hat and gloves, and with a stately tread was approaching the vestibule, when a slight bustle and whispering among the clerks arrested his steps.

'What is the matter?' asked he, turning round. 'I hope these are not sounds of contention I hear.'

'No,' said a broad, carroty-locked young man of a most pugnacious aspect, 'but—but—your lordship has forgotten that—that—'

'That what?' asked the marquis, rather impatiently.

'Oh! Merely that this afternoon is a half-holiday—and—and—'

'I understand,' replied his superior, smiling, 'you need not task your modesty with further explanation, Flannagan; the truth is, I suppose, you want your usual largess. I am obliged to you for reminding me—will that do?' he continued, as, opening his pocket-book, he took out a twenty-pound bank bill and laid it on the nearest desk.

'My lord, you are too generous', Flannagan began; but the chief secretary laughingly laid his gloved hand on his lips, and, with a condescending nod to the other clerks, sprang down the steps of the portico and strode hastily away, in order to escape the noisy expression of gratitude which now hailed his liberality.

On the opposite side of the long and wide street to that on which the splendid Home Office stands, rises the no less splendid Colonial Office; and, just as Arthur, Marquis of Douro, left the former structure, Edward Stanley Sydney departed from the latter: they met in the centre of the street.

'Well, Ned,' said my brother, as they shook hands, 'how are you to-day? I should think this bright sun and sky ought to enliven you if anything can.'

'Why, my dear Douro,' replied Mr. Sydney, with a faint smile, 'such lovely and genial weather may, and I have no doubt does, elevate the spirits of the free and healthy; but for me, whose mind and body are a continual prey to all the heaviest cares of public and private life, it signifies little whether sun cheer or rain damp the atmosphere.'

'Fudge', replied Arthur, his features at the same time assuming that disagreeable expression which my landlord denominates by the term *scorney*. 'Now don't begin to bore me, Ned, with trash of that description, I'm tired of it, quite: pray have you recollected that today is a half-holiday in all departments of the Treasury?'

'Yes; and the circumstance has cost me some money; these silly old customs ought to be abolished, in my opinion—they are ruinous.'

'Why, what have you given the poor fellows?'

'Two sovereigns.' An emphatic 'hem' formed Arthur's reply to this communication.

They had now entered Hotel Street and were proceeding in silence past the line of magnificent shops which it contains, when the sound of wheels was heard behind them and a smooth-rolling chariot dashed up and stopped just where they stood. One of the window-glasses now fell, a white hand was put out and beckoned them to draw near, while a silvery voice said, 'Mr. Sydney, Marquis of Douro, come hither a moment.'

Both the gentlemen obeyed the summons, Arthur with alacrity, Sydney with reluctance.

'What are your commands, fair ladies?' said the former, bowing respectfully to the inmates of the carriage, who were Lady Julia Sydney and Lady Maria Sneaky.

'Our commands are principally for your companion, my lord, not for you', replied the daughter of Alexander the First. 'Now Mr. Sydney', she continued, smiling on the senator, 'you must promise not to be disobedient.'

'Let me first know what I am required to perform', was the cautious answer, accompanied by a fearful glance at the shops around.

'Nothing of much consequence, Edward,' said his wife, 'but I hope you'll not refuse to oblige me this once, love. I only want a few guineas to make out the price of a pair of earrings I have just seen in Mr. Lapis's shop.'

'Not a bit of it', answered he. 'Not a farthing will I give you: it is scarce three weeks since you received your quarter's allowance, and if that is done already you may suffer for it.'

With this decisive reply, he instinctively thrust his hands into his breeches' pockets and marched off with a hurried step.

'Stingy little monkey!' exclaimed Lady Julia, sinking back on the carriage seat, while the bright flush of anger and disappointment crimsoned her fair cheek. 'This is the way he always treats me, but I'll make him suffer for it!'

'Do not discompose yourself so much, my dear', said her companion. 'My purse is at your service, if you will accept it.'

'I am sensible of your goodness, Maria, but of course I shall not take advantage of it; no, no, I can do without the earrings—it is only a fancy, though to be sure, I would rather have them.'

'My pretty cousin,' observed the marquis, who, till now, had remained a quiet though much amused spectator of the whole scene, 'you are certainly one of the most extravagant young ladies I know: why, what on earth can you possibly want with those trinkets? To my knowledge you have at least a dozen different sorts of ear-ornaments.'

'That is true, but then these are quite of another kind; they are so pretty and unique that I could not help wishing for them.'

'Well, since your heart is so much set upon the baubles, I will see whether my purse can compass their price, if you will allow me to accompany you to Mr. Lapis's.'

'Oh! thank you, Arthur, you are very kind', said Lady Julia, and both the ladies quickly made room for him as he sprang in and seated himself between them.

'I think,' said Maria Sneaky, who has a touch of the romp about her, 'I think when I marry I'll have just such a husband as you, my lord Marquis, one who won't deny me a pretty toy when I have a desire to possess it.'

'Will you?' said Arthur. 'I really think the Turks are more sensible people than ourselves.'

In a few minutes they reached the jeweller's shop. Mr. Lapis received them with an obsequious bow, and proceeded to display his glittering stores. The pendants which had so fascinated Lady Julia were in the form of two brilliant little humming-birds, whose jewelled plumage equalled if not surpassed the bright hues of nature. Whilst she was completing her purchase, a customer of a different calibre entered. This was a tall woman attired in a rather faded silk dress, a large bonnet, and a double veil of black lace which, as she lifted it on entering the shop, discovered a countenance which apparently had witnessed the vicissitudes of between thirty and forty summers. Her features might or might not have been handsome in youth, though they certainly exhibited slight traces of beauty now. On the contrary, a sharp nose, thin, blue lips, and flat eyebrows formed an assemblage of rather repulsive lineaments, even when aided by highly rouged cheeks and profusely frizzed dark locks.

One would have thought that such a person as I have described would have attracted but little attention from a young and gay nobleman like my brother. He, however, fixed his piercing eye upon her the moment she made her appearance. His gaze, nevertheless, did not indicate admiration, but rather curiosity and contempt; a keenly inquisitive expression, mingled with one of scorn, filled his countenance while he watched her.

With a slow and stiff movement she approached the counter, and addressing a shopman, desired to look at some rings. He instantly lifted the glass case and exposed to her view several hundreds of the articles she wanted. Deliberately the lady examined them all, but not one would suit. Diamonds, rubies, pearls, emeralds, topaz, etc. were each in their turn inspected and rejected. At length the shopman, who was a little out of patience at her extreme fastidiousness of choice, inquired what description of ring she could possibly want, since the first jeweller's depot in Verdopolis did not contain it.

'The ring I am in quest of', replied she, 'should be very small, of plain gold with a crystal stone, containing a little braided chestnut-coloured hair and this name (taking a scrap of paper from her reticule) engraven on the inside.'

'Well, madam,' answered he, 'we certainly have not just such an article as that in the shop at present, but we could very easily make one for you.'

'Could you finish it today?' asked she.

'Yes.'

'Then do so, and I will call for it this evening at nine o'clock.'

With these words she turned to leave the shop. Her eyes, as she lifted them from the counter, fell on the marquis and met his scrutinizing glance. For a moment she seemed to quail under its influence, but presently recovering herself, she dropped him a low curtsey, which was returned by a very slight and haughty bow, and sailed into the street.

'Who is that odd-looking woman?' asked Lady Julia as she drew on her gloves, after having finally completed her tedious bargain.

The marquis made no answer; but Maria Sneaky said, with an arch look, 'Some *ci-devant chère amie* of Douro's, I suppose; or perhaps a lady who will hereafter partake with me the benefit of a [illegible] matrimonial dispensation.'

'Is it so, Arthur?' inquired his cousin.

'Nay, Julia, I shall not tell you. You may draw your own inferences from the circumstances of the case.'

When he had assisted the ladies to their chariot, received his due tribute of parting smiles and thanks, and beheld the brilliant equipage roll merrily off, my brother turned down Hotel Street and directed his steps towards Victoria Square. A thoughtful and somewhat moody cloud darkened his brow as he entered Wellesley House, ascended the grand staircase, and proceeded through a succession of passages and chambers to the marchioness's apartment. On opening the door, and drawing aside the green damask curtain which hung within, he found her seated alone at a table and engaged in finishing a pencil sketch. She raised her head as he approached and welcomed him with a smile whose sweetness was more eloquent than words.

'Well, Marian,' said he, bending over her to look at the drawing, 'what is this you are about?'

'Only a little landscape, my lord, which I sketched in the valley yesterday.'

'It is really very pretty, and most charmingly pencilled; I think I remember the view. Is it not from the gateway of York Villa?'

'Yes, Arthur, and I have introduced Mr. Sydney in the foreground with a book in his hand.'

The marquis now sat down beside his wife and continued for some time silently watching the progress of her pencil. At length he recommenced the conversation by saying, 'Whom do you think I have seen in the city today, Marian?'

'I'm sure I don't know; perhaps Julius. I desired Mina to take him out for an airing about half an hour since.'

'No, you are far wrong in your guess.'

'Who, then?'

'None other than your old governess, Miss Foxley.'

At hearing this name, the colour faded from Marian's cheek. She paused in the midst of her employment, and slowly raising her large blue eyes from the paper, fixed them on Arthur with a look of deep alarm. He observed her agitation, and the thoughtful aspect of his countenance darkened into something like displeasure as he continued:

'What, Marian, is not that inexplicable spell yet broken? I thought absence and kind treatment might do much, but it appears all my affection has not yet succeeded in erasing that impression which, by some mysterious means, Miss Foxley contrived to make on your too sensitive mind.'

Tears now began to fill the marchioness's eyes and were dropping unheeded on her drawing as she answered, in a subdued tone, 'Do not be angry, Arthur.'

'I am not angry, Marian,' he replied, 'but can you deny that it was owing to that creature's cursed influence that you so long and steadfastly refused my hand, heart, and coronet—even when, as you have so often confessed, your inclination was not averse to the offer and when, as I could perceive, a final rejection would have blasted your happiness for life? Is it not from that cause that those transient periods of melancholy arise, with which you are even now oppressed?' Marian made no answer; he went on. 'How you at length summoned sufficient courage to throw off her shackles and consent to felicity I know not, nor is my penetration sufficiently keen to divine; but it appears there are yet some lingering remains of her power. Come, Marian, dismiss this weakness. How can she hurt you whilst under my protection? Make me your father confessor—you cannot find one more indulgent—and reveal all.'

Still there was no reply. The marquis now rose in anger. 'This is obstinacy, Marian,' he said, 'as well as weakness. I shall leave you for the present to reflect on the consequences of a continuance in such folly, but first let me warn you that I shall not suffer that woman to enter my house, or permit you to have any communication with her; and if I find my commands in this respect are disobeyed, I shall consider our interests as thenceforth separate. It is no part of my plan to allow the existence of a counteracting influence to my own in that heart and family where I ought to reign paramount.'

With these words he closed the door, and in a few minutes the echo of his retreating footsteps died away along the distant corridor.

It may perhaps be necessary to give my reader a more particular account of Miss Foxley before I proceed with my narrative. This I shall do in as few words as possible. She was the only child of a respectable merchant who died insolvent, leaving her an orphan, at the age of twenty-one, with no other fortune than her accomplishments—which were numerous—and her abilities—which, though not of the highest order, were nevertheless of a kind well fitted to enable her to push her way through the world, consisting chiefly in a capacity of discovering people's natural dispositions and adapting herself to them so as to worm a way into their good graces, and a certain sharp-sighted shrewdness wherever her own interests were concerned. In early youth she was not devoid of personal graces; but her beauty bore no proportion to her vanity, and any wound in that quarter never healed, but continued to fester till revenge in some tangible shape was achieved on the offending person. On her father's death, being unable to support herself in independence, she entered the family of the late Lady Hume in the situation of companion, and, as such, contrived so far to secure the confidence of that amiable and unsuspicious woman that on the birth of Marian she was appointed governess, for which office she was well qualified as far as talents and acquirements went. After Lady Hume's death, which took place when her daughter was fourteen years old, Miss Foxley still continued to reside at Sir Alexander's residence in Wellington's Land and was there when Arthur began to pay his addresses to her lovely young pupil. Unfortunately, the governess, who had now numbered her thirty-fifth year, was prompted by her unextinguishable vanity to imagine that she yet possessed charms potent enough to attract the admiration of a handsome and high-born nobleman. Under the influence of this delusion, she employed every art to draw away my brother's affections from the little unsophisticated girl who, in her opinion, knew not how to appreciate their value. Her efforts, however, were unsuccessful; they excited disgust instead of love; and at length, one afternoon when she was even more than usually forward, Arthur plainly though politely intimated that she was rather too old and obscure to form a fit wife for him. This was sufficient to kindle all the bad passions in Miss Foxley's mind. She vowed mentally to make him regret his cold and scornful rejection, and thenceforth set herself sedulously to work in order to prevent his union with her beautiful and youthful rival.

The effect of her endeavours soon became but too apparent. For some time Marian carefully avoided her noble lover, refused his hand, shunned his attentions, and so managed that Arthur, Marquis of Douro, the proudest and haughtiest youth of Verdopolis, was reduced to the condition of a pining, consumptive, lovesick young gentleman. Meantime, it was universally believed in the city that the delay of his union with the daughter of Sir Alexander Hume was owing to my father's opposition. How great would have been the surprise of all ranks had it been known by whom the objection was really started. It was evident, however, that Miss Hume's perseverance in this course was not unattended with pain to herself: her wan looks, attenuated form, and tearful eyes soon proclaimed that there was a wasting worm within. Still, however, she constantly refused to listen to my brother's passionate professions; and the triumph of Miss Foxley's intrigues was nearly completed when one day Arthur, having resolved to make a last attempt and then give up in despair, arrived at Badey Hall; to his astonishment he was at once shown into Marian's drawing-room, where he found her alone. What eloquent arguments he made use of to plead his cause, I know not; certain it is, however, that he was this time successful; and three weeks after, his lovely tyrant, amidst smiles, tears, and blushes, pledged her troth to him at the high altar [of St. Michael's] Cathedral. The first act of his authority as a husband was to command the immediate dismissal of Miss Foxley, who was consequently turned to the right about. He subsequently attempted to win from Marian an explanation of the causes which had so long delayed his happiness; but on this subject she maintained a mysterious silence; and he had for some time ceased to trouble her about it, till the governess's reappearance brought it again most unpleasantly to his memory.

CHAPTER THE IInd

When the marquis was gone, Marian, with a deep sigh, bent again over her half-finished picture; but now the pencil seemed to have lost its power, or the hand which directed it its skill. Instead of the flowing, correct lines and soft shadows which she had before produced, tremulous, wavering strokes and dark blotches mocked her unavailing efforts. At last she relinquished the attempt, and after replacing the sketch in her portfolio and closing the ivory box which contained her drawing materials, she drew towards her a harp which stood near. At first her slender, snowy fingers only extracted a few melancholy though sweet notes from the quivering strings; but soon these unconnected sounds gave place to a melody simple yet exquisitely plaintive; and ere long the according tones of her flutelike voice changed it to a delicious harmony while she sang the following little metrical fragment:

> On the shore of the dark, wild sea,
> Alone I am roaming,
> While sounds its voice mournfully
> Through the dim gloaming.
>
> O! those deep, hollow tones
> Sad thoughts inspire,
> They swell like the thrilling moans
> From breeze-swept lyre.

Echoes from rock and cave,
Solemnly dying,
Answer the howling wave,
Mock the wind's sighing.

Far in the silent sky,
Wandering worlds quiver;
Thus they shall beam on high,
Changeless for ever.

But ere another moon
Silvers the billow,
Ocean will be my tomb,
Sea-sand my pillow.

Then my unhallowed name
None shall remember:
Gone like the dying flame,
Quenched like the ember.

There were yet two verses of the fragment unsung, when she was interrupted by a rap at the door.

'Come in', said the marchioness, and Mina entered, carrying a lovely infant.

'Well, my darling', exclaimed she, as with an assumed expression of cheerfulness she rose and held out her arms to receive the pretty scion. 'How are you after your walk?'

'The fresh air has brought a little colour into his cheeks, my lady', replied Mina, relinquishing her charge.

'I see it has, and since that is the case, you had better take him out daily for the future, Mina.'

'Yes, I shall, my lady', replied the waiting-maid, seating herself at a small work-table and taking up a white robe which she previously had been embroidering for her mistress.

Marian for a few minutes continued talking to her little Julius and endeavouring to amuse him with the coral and gold bell suspended round his waist; but soon sad thoughts seemed to come over her mind, for she ceased to speak and sat gazing on the child with eyes of mournful meaning. Mina, who is a shrewd, penetrating girl, firmly attached to the marchioness and high in her confidence, presently perceived this depression of spirits, and desirous to learn the cause of it, she broke silence by saying, 'I fear something has happened to vex my lord.'

'What makes you think so?' asked Marian, starting.

'Because when I met him on the strand a little while since, he neither spoke to me nor Lord Julius, as he always does if he is in a good temper, but passed on with a grave and sorrowful look, though the little darling cried to go to him.'

To these words the marchioness made no reply, and Mina, resuming her work, continued to trace the rich pattern in silence. They continued thus employed for about half an hour, when a second rap was heard at the door. Mina rose to open it; a footman stood without with a letter.

'Who brought this, William?' asked his lady, after a hasty glance at the seal and direction.

'A little boy, my lady, who said that it had been given him by a woman in Harley Street.'

'Is he gone?'

'Yes, ma'am.'

'Very well, William, that will do.'

Hurriedly Marian broke the seal and ran over the contents of the letter. Her features whitened while she read, and at the conclusion it dropped from her nerveless hands. She would have fallen to the ground, had not the ready Mina been in an instant at her side. Happily she did not faint. On the contrary, a few minutes restored the vanishing rose to her cheek and lip. She then desired to be left alone. 'You may carry your work, Mina, into my dressing-room', said she. 'Take Julius to his nurse. Let no one come here till I ring the bell. I wish to be undisturbed for a short time.'

Mina accordingly withdrew, and it was midnight before she was again summoned to attend her lady. All the other servants had retired to rest an hour before, and she alone remained in the deserted hall, anxiously awaiting the expected sound. At length, just as she had formed the resolution to go uncalled, twelve o'clock struck and the wished-for tinkle sounded.

On opening the sitting-room door, she saw the marchioness placed exactly as she had left her, in a chair near the hearth, resting her head against the mantle-piece. There was no candle in the apartment, and in the grate the last feeble embers were just expiring.

'Will you not go upstairs now, my lady?' asked Mina. 'I have brought your bedroom lamp.'

'No, Mina, not yet. But come in, I want to speak to you.'

The waiting-maid closed the door and sat down in a chair which her mistress pointed out. Marian then continued, 'You know the marquis, Mina, as well as I do, and that being almost perfect himself, he cannot brook imperfection in others. His word and command have hitherto been my law, to which I have always submitted myself with cheerfulness and pleasure. Tonight, however, I am going to set in direct opposition to his will. Utter necessity must plead my excuse for such otherwise unpardonable disobedience; but if he discovers it, I am lost. Do you know where Harley Street is, Mina? I must go there this night.'

'No, my lady, I do not; but surely you do not intend to go alone?'

'Yes, I do.'

'That cannot be, my lady. You would be lost in the city. Do let my father go with you; he knows every street and lane of Verdopolis.'

'Is he in the house?'

'Yes, my lord ordered him to sleep here every night.'

'Call him, then.'

Mina left the room and in about ten minutes returned accompanied by her father.

Ned halted at the door for a moment. 'Come in, Edward', said the marchioness in her sweet, mild tone.

'I was only stripping my shoes, my lady,' said he, ''cause they're not fit to walk on such a grand carpet as this.'

'Oh, never mind that', replied she with a faint smile at his punctilious decorum. 'I am sorry to have called you from your bed, Edward, but I wished to learn from you what quarter of the city Harley Street is situated in.'

'Harley Street? Why, it's the same as they call Paradise Street, my lady, 'cause there's a house in it that you wouldn't like to pass by yourself at this time of night.'

'Should I not? Then will you go with me?'

'That I will, with all the pleasure in life.'

'Fetch my hat and cloak, then, Mina.'

'Had you not better take mine, my lady?' asked the prudent *fille de chambre*.

'Yes, on second thought that would certainly be the best.'

Mina again left the room and shortly came back with a plain straw hat and brown silk mantle. In these she attired her young mistress, and then, after lighting the fair adventurer and her guide down a private staircase to a street door, of which she possessed the key, returned to the servants' hall, and stretching herself on a [chintz] sofa that stood at the side of the still blazing hearth, was soon buried in a profound sleep.

The night was wild and stormy; vast, billowy clouds, from which a drizzling rain incessantly distilled, rolled over the sky, and at times, as they parted their folds, the serene moon was revealed shining far beyond them. A chill north wind mingled its moaning with that of the troubled sea, whose howling waves might now be heard uttering their voice afar off. With a light step and beating heart, Marian trod the wet, gloomy streets, preceded by her trusty conductor. After passing through many wide squares and long, broad streets, they entered a dark lane which would scarcely admit more than four persons abreast. On one side a line of lofty buildings arose, in the centre of which a sudden burst of moonlight discovered a flight of steps surmounted by a portico.

'This is Harley Street, my lady', said Ned, stopping and turning [illegible] around.

'Is it, Edward?' replied she in a low tone; and then, as if seized with a sudden agitation, she sank on the steps before mentioned.

Scarcely had she sat there for five minutes, when the sound of many footsteps was heard approaching. All was now again dark, so that nothing could be distinguished; but as the persons drew near, Marian easily recognized several by their voices.

'I think, vice-president, we are late tonight', said one in a deep, calm tone.

'Yes, most worthy [illegible]', was the reply, uttered in a voice which struck chill dismay to the marchioness's heart and caused her instantly to take refuge behind a sort of projecting pillar. 'Yes, we are, and I'll wager ten to one that Gordon proposes to fine us for it.'

'Taken, my lord Marquis', exclaimed another.

'Is that O'Connor?' asked the former speaker.

'Yes.'

'Done, then, and I hope to fleece you well, my most excellent knight of the mattock.'

Here the door within the vestibule opened and a sudden glare of lamps streamed on the dense, dark night, revealing the forms of about twenty of thirty gentlemen, most of them tall handsome men.

> Pride in their port, defiance in their eye,
> These mighty lords of human-kind passed by.*

Tumultuously they sprang or rushed up the steps into a vast and magnifi-

---

* Cf. Oliver Goldsmith, *The Traveller*: "Pride in their port, defiance in their eye,/I see the lords of human kind pass by" (ll. 327–28).

cent hall, blazing with sunlike chandeliers which appeared above. Then the door closed and night reassumed her solemn, silent reign.

'Those are rare young chaps', said Ned, as he rejoined the terrified marchioness. 'If they had seen you, there would have been some'at to do; only his lordship was there, and that would have [illegible] checked them a bit, I guess.'

'Let us proceed now, Edward', said she.

'Which house are we to stop at, my lady?'

'The last in the street, on the left hand.'

They soon reached it, and Marian, after directing Ned to wait on the outside till she should return, knocked timidly at the door. It was presently opened by a dirty-looking servant wench in a dingy lace cap and gaudy cotton gown.

'Is there not a lady of the name of Miss Foxley lodging here?' asked the marchioness.

'Yes, madam, and if you'll follow me I'll show you her apartment.' Accordingly, after carefully fastening the door, she led the way up a narrow flight of stone steps and through a sort of lobby, which was dimly lighted by a single lamp, to a room at the further end. Entering first, she announced that the lady was come.

'Indeed', said someone within; 'bring her here directly'; and the visitor was ushered into a small chamber, whose furniture consisted of a mahogany pembroke table, five or six cane-bottomed chairs, a scanty carpet, faded green window curtains, and a broken paper screen. A small but bright fire burned in the grate, and beside it a tall female was seated in an armchair. She rose as Marian entered and advanced to meet her, saying, 'My lady Marchioness, how are you? I am surprised at your condescension in deigning to visit so obscure an individual as myself. Pray be seated, if these poor chairs are not too mean to support a peeress of the realm.'

'Miss Foxley,' replied the marchioness, as she took the offered seat, 'I have run considerable risk in complying with your request; nor am I sure that my conduct in this respect is right; but my anxiety to learn the truth of what your letter hinted at induced me to disregard all other considerations. Pray give me a more explicit account without delay.'

'Why, madam!' returned the governess, with a fiendlike smile. 'You are doubtless now a happy wife, loving and beloved. The marquis, by all accounts, makes a fond husband; and a son, I understand, has lately crowned your felicity. But, my lady, is not this bliss too perfect to endure?

Do you not dread an interruption? A profound calm is generally succeeded by a storm. Do you not know of one whose appearance would utterly blast all this course of ecstatic pleasure?'

'Miss Foxley, Miss Foxley,' murmured Marian, in a scarcely audible tone, 'don't torture me so, for heaven's, for my mother's sake, whom you once respected. End this suspense and let me know the worst. Is he returned?'

'I will show you', answered Miss Foxley, ringing the bell, which was almost instantly answered by the servant-maid. 'Tell the gentleman in the next room I wish to speak with him', said she.

The girl departed, and almost immediately after a young man entered the room. He was tall and genteelly formed, with brown hair, wild dark eyes, and a handsome though meagre countenance.

'Mr. Henry,' said Miss Foxley, 'allow me to introduce your early friend, Marian Hume, to you. [Now,] unfortunately, she bears another surname, but that is not my fault.'

He approached the marchioness, who sat with her face buried in her hands, and said, 'Madam, permit me to announce myself as that long-absent Henry Percy, who once, at least, was honoured with your regard.'

At the sound of his voice, she raised her head, looked at him fixedly for some minutes, and then replied, 'This is not, cannot be Henry. He was younger, fairer, his voice softer. Miss Foxley, you are deceiving me; this person scarcely resembles him in the least.'

'That may be', answered the governess, 'yet, notwithstanding, he is Henry Percy, your Henry Percy, and no other.'

'I deny it, here is his picture (taking a portrait from her bosom). Compare them and tell me where the similitude lies.'

'Madam,' interposed the young man, 'I do not wonder at your denial of my identity. The lapse of time and a long sojourn in foreign climates must necessarily have produced a vast change; but though I may be altered externally, yet within all is as it ever was, which is, I fear, more than can be said of some other.'

'Do not insult me, sir', said Marian, the deadly white to which her cheek had faded giving place to a bright flush of anger. 'I shall believe the evidence of my senses, rather than your assertions.'

'Since you will not credit my word,' replied he, 'look at this token, and reject its testimony if you dare.'

So saying, he put into her hand a small silver box. She opened it: a single glance at its contents seemed to bring sudden and forcible conviction; for with a faint shriek she sank back in the chair, almost deprived of animation.

'Now, perjured one, do you acknowledge me?' asked Mr. Percy with bitter emphasis.

'I do, I do, but oh! spare me for one week: give me at least that time for thought, for consideration.'

'Not a day, not an hour will I spare you! My claim is legal and I will enforce it now.'

The marchioness then fell on her knees, and with streaming eyes and clasped hands implored a reprieve, however short. Her extreme agony seemed at length to move him.

'Rise, madam', said he. 'You shall have a week's delay, on condition that you promise not to consult with the Marquis of Douro during that time.'

'And', added Miss Foxley, 'on condition that you likewise promise to return here tomorrow night in order to receive important information respecting yourself, my lady, which you do not at present appear to be in a situation to listen to.'

'I will promise anything!' exclaimed she, grateful for this temporary relief. 'But of what nature is the information you allude to, Miss Foxley?'

'I merely wish to let you know who and what you are, a circumstance of which you have hitherto been ignorant.'

'Cannot I hear it now?'

'No, it is too late, and the dawn is already rising.'

Marian, then, after some further conversation, took her leave. She found Ned anxiously awaiting her return in the street by the dim light of the breaking day. They hastily trod the path to Wellesley House, where, fortunately, they arrived unobserved. Ned, then, after receiving his young lady's cordial thanks, which he valued even more than the solid reward which accompanied them, retired to enjoy in peace the refreshment of undisturbed slumber. The marchioness likewise sought her pillow; but sorrow and sad thought banished sleep far from the stately couch where she lay.

CHAPTER THE IIIrd

On the night after that spoken of in my last chapter, the drawing-room at Ellrington House exhibited a more tranquil scene than it usually does. Instead of the dark political [design], turbulent and boisterous wine party, or [dazzling and bewildering] crowd of Fashion's bright devotées, two persons alone, the lord and lady of the mansion, sat one on each side of the cheerful and tranquil hearth. A few wax tapers on the mantel piece, shining amongst a hundred sparkling decorations aided by the blaze of a clear fire, furnished light sufficient to enable Lord Ellrington to peruse a treatise on the present state of society, and his wife to decipher the characters of a Persian poem. At length the former, after several muttered expressions of contempt for his author, threw down the work and said, 'Come, Zenobia, give up poring over that absurd [passion] you are at there. I dare say, if one could read it, it's the rarest trash in nature.'

'Indeed, Ellrington, you are mistaken; finer sentiments were never embodied in language. But what book have you been reading all this time?'

'A translation into the English tongue of an ass's bray.'

'Indeed? Then you were less profitably employed than myself. I was construing the song of a nightingale to his favourite rose.'

'And pray, what is the name of the idiot who has conceived that surpassingly magnificent idea?'

'[Ferdoona], one of the greatest poets Persia ever produced.'

'And do you really, Zenobia, admire such groveling nonsense?'

'Most undoubtedly I do.'

'Well, women are the most incomprehensible creatures on earth; sometimes you seem to be possessed of considerable sense and discernment, and then again you commit acts and utter speeches which argue a great weakness, if not a total deprivation, of intellect.'

'Granting it is so, Alexander: might I not say the same of you? How often during the revolution of a year are you as rational as at present?'

'If I were not in a particularly easy humour tonight that sentence would stick in my throat, Zenny.'

'Would it? And most likely, in that case, a bottle of wine would be necessary to wash it down.'

'Probably, but tell me, now I think on it, what makes you hide all your hair under that singularly formed cap which you have lately worn?'

'Fashion, my lord, and the caprice of custom.'

'What? Does Fashion induce the ladies to destroy their beauty?'

'Sometimes, but since you dislike it, the defect is easily remedied.' So saying, she plucked out the comb which confined her hair, and immediately a cloud of raven tresses fell down in rich profusion over her neck and shoulders.

'There,' said Ellrington after a moment's silence, 'you look like yourself, now. It is astonishing what a difference the presence or absence of a few curled locks makes.'

Pleased with her attention to his wishes, he found himself in a better and more amicable humour than any which had soothed his stormy soul for many a long year, when, just as he had reached the acme of suavity, a rap was heard at the door.

'Come in', said he, and the servant who stood without was startled at the gentleness of tone in which these words were pronounced, as generally, when he ventured to disturb his master thus, a volley of oaths and curses formed the reward of his pains. Timidly opening the door, he announced that a person wished to speak with Lord Ellrington.

'A person! And pray, what kind of a one is it, coming here at this time of night?'

'It is a woman, my lord, and, I believe, a young one, though she keeps her face so covered with a handkerchief that I can't see it distinctly.'

'Hey! some mystery! Well, show her into the library and say I'll come directly.'

'What can the creature possibly want?' said Lady Zenobia. 'I think, Ellrington, it was foolish of you not to send a denial.'

'Oh! nonsense, Zenny. She may have something particular to tell me, you know.'

When Lord Ellrington entered the library, he perceived a slender female figure attired in a silk mantle and a large straw hat which had fallen back and discovered a luxuriant flow of beautiful chestnut ringlets. Her face was turned away and partially hidden with the palms of her small white hands.

'Well, my girl,' said he, 'what is your business with me?'

At first she made no answer. He repeated the question. She then slowly lifted her head and discovered a countenance which, bright with blushes and formed in the most exquisite mould of youthful loveliness, appeared an object so fair and fascinating that the lofty nobleman could not restrain an exclamation of surprise. After gazing at her a moment with an astonished air, he said, 'Do I deceive myself, or is this the peerless Marchioness of Douro?'

'My lord, your conjecture is right', replied she, at once seeming to throw off the bashfulness which had before oppressed her and fearlessly meeting his fixed gaze with an eye that sparkled almost with the light of insanity. 'I am that unhappy woman.'

'And to what am I indebted for this unexpected, though most welcome, pleasure?'

'To desperation, my lord. Nothing short of that should have made me humble myself so.'

'I am sorry for that, fair lady, as I hoped you were come of free will; but tell me, in what I can serve you? It shall not be said that the prettiest woman in Verdopolis asked my assistance in vain.'

'Do not talk so, Lord Ellrington', exclaimed Marian, while a sudden shudder ran through her whole frame. 'Knowing what I know, such light language sounds horrible.'

'And what do you know, my lady?'

'What I would not tell you for worlds and what I am come here in order to confirm, though I fear it scarce needs confirmation.'

'This is mysterious language, I do not understand it.'

'But you will ere long. Tell me, my lord, have you not a casket belonging to the late Lady Percy, which up to this day you have never been able to open?'

'I have, but how in the name of the heavens, the earth, the seas, and all that are therein did you obtain knowledge of it?'

'That I cannot explain to you at present, my lord. Permit me only to see the box, and I will show you a method of opening it.'

'Well, I really cannot refuse a request from such lips, so permit me, my lady Marchioness, to conduct you into the apartment where the object of your curiosity is kept.' With these words, he offered to take her hand. She, however, withdrew it with an apparently involuntary movement of repulsion.

'What?' said he, scowling furiously, 'do you dare to reject in disdain that courtesy which it was almost a condescension for me to offer?'

'I was wrong', replied Marian, bursting into tears. 'You may take my hand, Lord Ellrington, for I fear you have a right to command me in everything.'

The last words were uttered in so low a tone as to be inaudible to his lordship. Her tears, however, softened him, as he imagined them to arise from a dread of his anger. He therefore accepted the hand which otherwise might perhaps now have been declined, and taking up a candle, led her out of the room.

They passed in silence across the entrance hall, ascended the grand staircase, and trod with noiseless step the matted floor of a long gallery, at the termination of which was a door. This Lord Ellrington unlocked, and they entered a small apartment panelled with black oak. In the centre of it stood a table covered with papers and in one corner an elaborately carved cabinet in which lay four swords, three sheathed and one naked. Above them hung a large banner, blood-red and bearing for its device a skull and cross-bones in black.

'This', said the nobleman, after having again locked the door, 'is my *sanctum sanctorum*, lady Marchioness.' He paused and looked steadily upon her, as if to see what impression the scene produced.

It was indeed a strangely awful situation for poor Marian to be placed in. There she stood at the dead hour of the night, alone and face to face with that dark, stern man whose mighty talents and still mightier crimes will hereafter appall the muse of history as she records them. A deep and boding silence reigned around, interrupted only by the faint, dull sound of a closing door [or] hurried tread from some distant part of the vast mansion, sounds that only served to intimate that help, if needed, was too far off to be obtained. Cold ran the blood to that youthful lady's heart as she thought on these things, but terror so restrained her tongue and fettered her limbs while under the influence of that searching falcon eye, that she neither breathed a word nor moved a finger.

'How do you like it?' he continued with a sardonic smile, lifting the lamp and drawing up his lofty form to all its majestic height. 'You see those four swords and that red flag on the cabinet yonder?'

She bowed.

'Well, now, my lady, I'll tell you what they mean. This is the blade I wielded in my youth, when I killed Negroes for Wellington. This is the weapon that helped me in exile; it is drunk with the blood of merchants by sea and land. And [this] not many years since, made Alexander the First tremble on his mountain throne. Those three are all sheathed; they have done their work, they have slain their thousand and tens of thousands and now they may rest. But for this other! Look at it, my lady, look at it well. See how sharp and bright and glittering it is—not a spot of blood, not a streak of rust blackens it. This is a virgin sword, it has pierced no heart, freed no spirit; but it lies bare and ready; it bides its time. A voice and a power is in that weapon: the voice shall speak the doom of nations; the power shall execute it. And by the strength of what arm shall it do these things?' he continued, suddenly laying his hand on her shoulder with a force that made her tremble. 'And for what prize will the great game be played? Mine is the arm, a crown is the prize!'

He paused a moment, and then went on again in a lower tone. 'As for that flag, it is the pennon of the Black Rover. For seven years it swept the seas, the dreaded, the invincible. In storm and sunshine, war and mirth, the battle and the festival, she remained unhurt, unchanged. When the waves were strewed with the tempest-torn fragments of the merchantman and the man-of-war, my good ship, their dread and scourge, spread her white sail and, like a haunting spirit of the deep, proudly breasted those waters that none else dared look upon. Men said she was charmed against wind and wave, and they spoke truth; for I trod her deck and directed her course, therefore Destiny with her triple shield ever hovered round—

'But stop! Am I a madman or an idiot, to talk thus to you? Humph! I fear I have been letting out. But it is easy to prevent consequences. Kneel down, my Marchioness of Douro, kneel this instant. Dare you resist? There, that is right. You must excuse the push I gave you, but it is always best to obey me at once without hesitation. Now swear by the head of that old man whom you worship never to whisper in mortal ear one word of what I have been saying this night. Swear, or—'

'I do swear', said she in a faint voice.

'That is well. Get up. You are an obedient and praiseworthy girl, and if I had the management of you would soon arrive at the perfection of feminine meekness and humility.'

Marian rose and stood before the imperious nobleman. She was deadly pale and might have passed for a beautiful marble statue, had not the tremor which shook every limb indicated that her form was of living flesh and blood. Lord Ellrington again fixed his eye on her and seemed to take pleasure in witnessing the profound awe which his keen gaze inspired. At last, after torturing her thus for some minutes, he broke out into a long and loud burst of laughter. She stepped back and looked at him doubting-ly, as if she thought his brain disturbed.

'Well,' he exclaimed as soon as the exhaustion arising from his strange fit of merriment would permit him to speak, 'have I frightened you, my lady? Come! nonsense! cheer up! One would think you were never spoken to harshly or looked at sternly before. Pray, does the marquis never discipline you a little in this way? Confess the truth now, is he not sometimes rather crusty and overbearing?'

'My lord,' stated Marian, while an indignant blush crimsoned her snowy brow and faded cheek, 'I will not hear my husband's name mentioned thus, even by you, satanically proud as you are—' She would have said more, but the half-formed words died away on her lips, and with them the transient flash of spirit likewise vanished.

'Satanically proud', muttered Lord Ellrington after her. 'That is daring. You forget, I think, my lady, where you are and how situated; but methinks you need not pretend to be so thin-skinned as it regards the marquis at the moment when you are committing what in his eyes would unquestionably appear a most deadly offence; for I do not think he is acquainted with this midnight visit to Ellrington House.'

Marian made no reply to this cutting remark; she only sighed deeply. A pause now ensued, during which Lord Ellrington slowly paced the room. It was some time before she ventured to interrupt him by again referring to the business which had occasioned her visit. At length, summoning resolution, she said hesitatingly, 'Can your lordship permit me to look at the casket now?'

Without answering, he strode directly to the cabinet and, taking a key from his pocket, unlocked it. A multitude of miscellaneous articles were contained in the different divisions; but in one, more carefully arranged than the rest, there appeared an ivory box inlaid with silver, a long braided lock of beautiful light-brown hair, a lady's watch, and a miniature portrait of a beautiful woman set in a massive gold frame, richly decorated with jewels. He took the box and put it into her hand.

She moved a few paces from him towards the table on which the lamp was placed, and having opened the casket by means of a secret spring, took from it a paper that formed the whole of its contents. This she glanced hastily over, and then, suddenly and before Lord Ellrington could prevent her, consumed it in the flame of the lamp, exclaiming when she had done, 'Thank God that evidence is destroyed.'

'How dare you?' said he, approaching her with angry strides and laying his hand, as if by instinct, on a pistol which appeared half-hidden in his breast. 'If you were a man I'd blow you to atoms for that action this moment.'

'Do it now', said Marian, perfectly undaunted by his manner, 'and rid me of a life which I have lost the power of enjoying.'

'No,' he replied, thrusting back the pistol, 'I'll not kill you, but I'll do what perhaps in your present state of mind would be almost as bad. I'll keep you locked up here till you tell me, and that truly, the contents of the paper which you have just destroyed.'

'That I will never do; every fresh view which I obtain of your conduct determines me more against it.'

'Is the silly girl mad?' said Lord Ellrington with a gloomy frown. 'Has she forgotten who and what I am?'

'No, my lord, I have not; but the sentiments which I cannot help entertaining against you will force their way despite of all my efforts to restrain them.'

'[Note], then, you may take the consequences of your want of self-government, and continue here with me at least till the morning light. If you behave well during the next five or six hours, I may perhaps permit you to return home in [time] to explain your absence to the marquis as you best can.'

In vain did Marian endeavour by entreaties, remonstrances, and even tears, to turn him from his purpose. He was inexorable; and during the remainder of that night, she was compelled to continue an unwilling prisoner, listening to the keen taunts, false insinuations, and detested gallantry of her stern jailer. At last, just as the lamp was beginning to wane before the first pale beams of dawn which shone faintly through the single lofty and narrow window with which the apartment was lighted, a hesitating knock was heard at the door.

'Who's there?' thundered Lord Ellrington.

'It is only I', replied the voice of his wife, in very subdued tones. 'I wished to know, Alexander, whether you intended to retire to rest at all before morning or not.'

'And how dare you wish to know anything about the matter? Off to your bed this instant, without reply!' Zenobia understood the accent in which her husband spoke and withdrew immediately.

'Now,' said he, turning to the marchioness, 'I will allow your little ladyship to depart. Come along.'

Gladly she followed him as, after unlocking the door, he led the way through gallery, hall, and passage to the grand entrance. This he unfastened with his own hands. Marian did not wait for any farewell ceremonies, but darting past him, cleared the steps at a spring, fled down the street with the speed and lightness of a roe, and was out of sight in a twinkling. An effusion of golden light filled the east before she reached Wellesley House. All, however, was still silent around that lordly mansion; and when she rung the bell at the private door it was opened by Mina.

'Oh, my lady,' exclaimed that faithful handmaiden, 'I am so glad you are come. I have passed such a night of suspense and misery on your account as no one ever did before, scarcely.'

'Did the marquis return home last night?' asked her mistress.

'Yes, he did at four o'clock. I then thought that your absence could not miss being discovered and gave up all for lost; but most fortunately he went to his own bedroom, and therefore everything is still safe, you know, my lady.'

'Thank Heaven and the Great Genii* who watched over me!' ejaculated the marchioness. 'Now, Mina, go to bed, as I am sure you must be tired. I can undress myself.'

---

* The Genii were the four Brontë children. Cf. Wise and Symington, 8:61.

64

Mina then left the room, and in a few minutes her young mistress, oppressed with grief and watching, was enjoying a temporary oblivion of her sorrows in the repose of sleep.

CHAPTER THE IVth

She had scarcely rested three hours when Mina again stood by her bedside. 'My lady,' said she, 'will you rise now? The marquis has sent up to say that breakfast is waiting.'

'What o'clock is it?' asked Marian.

'Nine, my lady.'

'Oh! then I will rise, of course. How provoking that he should have to wait for me!'

The marchioness was soon dressed, as her attire in the morning is dictated by the very spirit of tasteful simplicity; and a few touches brought her soft, naturally curling glossy tresses into becoming order. When the business of the toilette was over, she proceeded to attend the marquis. Her heart beat fast as she approached the breakfast-room, for she had not seen him since the interview mentioned in one of my former chapters, when he left her in anger, sternly prohibiting any intercourse with Miss Foxley—and how had this prohibition been attended to?

Arthur, as she entered the apartment, was seated with his back to the door, engaged in the perusal of a newspaper. Her tread was too light to attract attention; and she feared to address him unspoken to, uncertain whether he had yet forgotten his wrathful mood; so she quietly took her seat at the table and began to arrange the material for breakfast.

The tinkle of porcelain and silver soon roused him; he looked up with a smile and said, 'Well, Marian, won't you bid me good morning? I hope you are not in a bad temper at being called out of your bed so early.'

'No, indeed, Arthur, on the contrary. I am ashamed of myself for having made you wait so long. Forgive me, however, as I am not often so deficient in punctuality.'

'I'll consider about [it]', replied he playfully. 'Perhaps your request may be granted, for I do not find myself inclined to be very angry on that score.'

My brother's breakfast is generally protracted to the space of about an hour and a half, as instead of eating straightforward, like other people, he sits maundering over the morning papers and, as my landlord says, taking a sup and a bite at intervals of about a quarter of an hour each. Some ladies of my acquaintance would raise a fine hubbub if they had to wait for their husbands such an unconscionable length of time; but the Marchioness of Douro, who considers herself honoured in being permitted to attend the beck of her lord and master when she has finished her own slight repast, usually takes up some piece of ornamental fancy-work and continues patiently plying the needle with her small, slight fingers until the last leading article of the last newspaper is concluded.

This morning, her labour was interrupted by frequent and deep sighs. Every time one of these indications of grief escaped her lips, the marquis, though unseen by his wife, just lifted his eyes from the paper and surveyed her with a most peculiar expression; and when they fell again on the speech or paragraph, he seemed for a moment rather engaged with his own thoughts than the sense of what he was reading. At length, like all sublunary things, Arthur's breakfast had an end; the service being cleared away and all set to rights by an attendant footman, Marian was about to leave the room in order to visit her nursery, when suddenly the marquis rose, and coming close up to her, took her hand.

'Marian,' said he after a momentary silence, 'you look very pale this morning. What is the reason of it?'

'I—I—did not sleep very well last night', stammered she, while her frame trembled like an aspen leaf.

'That is not all, it could not occasion this tremor. And what makes your hand turn so cold within mine?'

'I am sure I do not know', replied Marian, endeavouring to force a smile; but the attempt only brought a tear into her dark blue eye.

The marquis looked at her as if he would have pierced to the farthest recesses of her heart, and said in a low thrilling voice, 'Have you disobeyed my mandates? Have you seen that woman and are her chains again riveted round you?'

There was a pause. Marian seemed almost annihilated; the rapidly varying hue of her countenance proclaimed the violence of those emotions with which her soul was now rent. She could not answer, she could not even look up at her imperious lord, but stood voiceless and motionless like one petrified.

'It is well', said he, dropping her hand and sternly folding his arms. 'I understand that silence. You have chosen to follow the direction of your own weak inclinations and to disregard my wishes. I have told you before that the consequence of such a line of conduct would be an immediate separation. It is my custom to make my words and deeds conformable; therefore, this very day and before three hours elapse, the travelling-carriage will be in readiness to take you to my father's countryhouse in Wellington's Land. Good-bye. This is in all probability our last interview, for I cannot love a disobedient wife.'

'Arthur, my dearest Arthur, don't leave me thus! You would not think so hardly of me if you knew all!'

'Tell me all, then!' said he hastily, and taking his hand from the door-lock, which he was just about to turn.

'I dare not!'

'And why?'

'Because I am bound by a promise not to consult you for a week; and at the end of that time all consultation will, I fear, be in vain, for then I must leave you for ever.'

The marquis was going to answer, when the door opened and his Grace the Duke of Wellington entered. He halted, as Bobadil* would say, on the threshold, and after looking keenly from Arthur to Marian and noting the attitude and countenance of each, said in a quiet tone of inquiry, 'What ails you both? Have I arrived just in time to witness a slight specimen of matrimonial felicity, eh?'

There was no answer; the marquis only moved away to a window and began to watch the clouds as they sailed slowly by. His Grace then addressed himself more particularly to the lady. 'What have you done, Marian,' said he, 'to bring that lowering and tempestuous cloud over your husband's countenance?'

Marian burst into tears. 'I did not mean to offend him', sobbed she, 'but—but—'

'What, love? I trust this is not unnecessary severity on his part.'

'No, no, no, he only wishes to know something which I cannot tell him.'

'And what is that something? Can you tell me?'

'Yes', said the marchioness, looking up, while a smile began to illumine her still glistening eyes. 'I think I will. Your Grace will know how to advise me better than anyone else, and I have not promised to keep it a secret from you.'

'Come then, child; sit down by me and let us hear this wonderful secret.'

Marian sat down beside the duke as he desired her; for a little while she was silent and seemed to be collecting her faculties and summoning resolution for some great effort. The composure of resignation rather than

---

* The allusion is not clear, but the name occurs also in Branwell's "Letters from an Englishman", Wise and Symington, 8:102. Cf. Captain Bobadil in Ben Jonson's *Every Man in his Humour*.

peace at length overspread her features, but there was still a wildness in her look and a tremble in her voice as she said, 'My lord Duke, I am not your son's wife, I am not Sir Alexander Hume's daughter.'

At these words the Marquis of Douro started as if he had received a shock of electricity. He turned round and would have spoken, but his father restrained him, saying, 'Hush, Arthur, not a word from your lips or I shall desire you to quit the room instantly. Now my love,' he continued, addressing Marian, 'explain to me in the first place how you are not my son's wife.'

'About five years ago,' replied she, 'a short time before my mother, or her whom until lately I considered as such, died, and when she was fast wasting under that languishing disease which at length destroyed her, I was one day summoned to her chamber. She was sitting up supported by pillows, and near the bedside stood Mr. Hall, our private chaplain, Miss Foxley, my governess, whom your Grace may perhaps remember to have seen (the duke nodded assent) and Henry Percy, the youngest son of Lord Ellrington, whose country-seat was situated not far from Badey Hall. He was a boy about my own age, and had been my playfellow as long as I could remember.

'"Marian," said my mother when I came to her, "you have often heard me speak of the late Lady Percy, have you not?" I said I had, and she went on, "She was my dearest friend. All her wishes are now sacred to me, and there is one of them which this day I desire to see fulfilled. On her deathbed, shortly after you and Henry were born, she expressed a wish that, in remembrance of our friendship, you should be united in case of your both arriving at years of discretion. I am now dying, and tomorrow Henry will depart on a voyage to a distant part of the world, whence he may never return. I should like, therefore, to see you betrothed now in my presence, and if my always hitherto dutiful daughter would render her mother's last moments happy, she will consent to bestow her hand on one who I doubt not will hereafter render her a happy wife."

'I could not refuse to comply with my dear mother's request, when I knew how soon the grave and coffin were to hide her forever from my sight; and besides, even had the powerful motive of obedience to her been absent, I could have found no excuse in my own inclinations to sanction a refusal: though I did not then know what love was, yet I had always liked Henry Percy, who was a handsome and affectionate boy, for his good nature and kind disposition. We accordingly pledged our faith before the chaplain and each gave the other a token by which, when we met again at some future period, we might recognize each other. The next day he set out on his long journey, and a few weeks after my mother was carried to the tomb.

'Time passed on, and I heard nothing of Henry till the third year after his departure, when one morning Miss Foxley was looking over a newspaper in which she showed me a paragraph announcing the wreck of *The Mermaid*, the ship which Henry had sailed in, among some distant and unknown countries called the South Sea Islands, and the destruction of all her crew, including Lieutenant Percy, son of the celebrated Alexander Rogue. I mourned for Henry's death, but neither long nor bitterly. Absence had caused his image and the calm, childlike affection with which I viewed him to grow dim in my mind and memory.

'Twelve months after, I saw the marquis; new feelings, passions which I had never till then experienced, arose in my heart. I need not tell your Grace that all things were settled for my union with your son, when, in what must have appeared to you an unaccountably capricious manner, I suddenly stopped the preparations and declared that I never could consent to be his wife. I had, however, a reason, and one sufficiently conclusive. Three days before my marriage was to have taken [place], and while Miss Foxley was engaged in making my bridal dress, she received a letter from a shipmate of Henry's with whom she was acquainted, declaring that the story of *The Mermaid*'s wreck was all false and that both vessel and crew were well and pursuing a prosperous voyage.

'You cannot, my lord, I think blame me if after this, though with the greatest violence to my own feelings, I broke off all intercourse with your son. None can tell what I suffered when I saw him day by day pining for my sake, but Duty strongly pointed out to me the path which I ought to pursue, and I dared not turn aside. Your opinion of my caprice must have been confirmed, when after several months of steady rejection, I at once and suddenly yielded to his entreaties. There was a cause for this, but I scarcely dare tell it you lest you should suspect me of an inclination for romance.'

The duke encouraged her to continue, and she went on. 'Late one calm summer's evening, I wandered out to a distant part of the grounds, and sitting down in a little wild alcove which was my favourite retreat, began sorrowfully to brood over the image of Arthur and the sad certainty that I should never be his. I thought and wept till it began to grow dark; and then, fearful of passing through the park at night and disturbing the deer and wild cattle from their slumbers, I rose to return and had advanced a little way up the forest walk where the alcove was erected, when a voice, faint and mournful, whispered my name. I turned and saw, standing under the arch I had just left, the dim figure of a man.

'"Who is there?" I asked in some alarm.

'Instead of answering, he glided towards me. I shrieked out. He beckoned me to be silent and said, in very hollow tones which I shudder even now to recollect, "Look at me, Marian, and know your Henry."

'Just then the moon broke from a cloud, and her light, falling through the branches, revealed to me a form and face which bore, indeed, a slight resemblance to Henry; but it was so changed and distorted that I should never have recognized it of my own accord. The hair and clothes were all wet and dripping, the eyes wide open but void of all expression save one of ghastliness, the face blue and livid and all the features swollen. I was too much appalled at this horrid change to answer, and he [went on]:

'"So I lie, Marian, among the Coral Islands of the South Sea. Listen not to deceivers, fear not that I shall return. Death and the waters of a vast deep chain me to my place; be happy and think of your first love no more." The wraith then walked into air before me, and filled with horror, I hastened back to the house.

'On arriving there, I related what I had seen to Miss Foxley. She strongly endeavoured to persuade me that it was all the fruit of my own excited imagination; but, finding my belief in the reality of the apparition fixed, and likewise my determination to act according to its counsel, she grew angry and left me, saying she prayed that if I did marry the marquis, my repentance hereafter would be deep and bitter. Three weeks subsequent to this I was married. Arthur, shortly after our union, dismissed Miss Foxley, which I was very glad of, as her sullen looks and threatening [scowls] filled me with an undefined feeling of fear.

'Since that time I have received no intelligence of her till about two days ago, when the marquis informed me that he had seen her in the city and warned me against holding any communication with her. The same day a letter was brought me from her, saying that if I did not wish the whole of a certain transaction to come out, I would condescend, marchioness as I was, to visit my old governess at her lodgings in Harley Street. I went, for I dared not do otherwise, and there I saw that Henry Percy whom till then I had supposed buried in the sea.

'He was so changed, and looked so dark and wild and meagre, that at first I denied his identity; but I was soon but too well convinced by the production of that very token which five years since I had given him as a pledge of my eternal faith. He would have claimed his right over me that instant; by tears and entreaties I, however, gained a reprieve of a week, on condition that during that time I would not consult with my husband on the subject and that I would return to Harley Street next day in order to learn an important secret concerning myself.

'At the second interview, Miss Foxley informed me that I was not the daughter of Sir Alexander Hume!

'"Who, then?" I asked.

'"The late Ladies Hume and Percy", she replied, "were, as you know, most intimate friends. As a sign of their love for and confidence in each other, they agreed, when you and Henry were born, to exchange children and each bring up the other's child as their own. The affair was managed so dexterously that none but myself knew anything of it; and till this moment you have looked up to Dr. Hume as your father, when in reality no less a person than Lord Ellrington stands in that relation to you."

'This information affected me so deeply that I fainted. On recovering, I told Miss Foxley that, unless she could bring proof of her assertion, I should consider all I had just heard in the light of a malignant falsehood. She then informed me that there was a written agreement of the affair enclosed in a casket of Lady Percy's, which was fastened by a secret spring [concealed] in a particular part, which she described to me; and that most probably, from the difficulty of discovering this spring, Lord Ellrington yet retained the box unopened.

'Half-maddened by the idea of being that man's child whom of all others I most dreaded and detested, I went, scarcely knowing what I did, to Ellrington House. There, by entreaties, I prevailed on his lordship to show me the casket. I opened it, found the fatal document, glanced over its contents, and in a moment of anguish, consumed it in the flame of a candle which stood on the table.

'Now, my lord,' she continued, 'you know all my secret, and may, if you can, fathom the depth and weigh the burden of that misery under which my reason at times seems to totter. I hate explanation, and therefore shall condense what I have further to say into as brief a space as possible.'

When Marian had finished, the marquis asked her to describe to him the token by which she had recognized Henry Percy.

'It was', replied she, 'a small gold ring with a crystal stone containing a little of my hair braided, and my name written on the inside.'

'The vile old witch!' exclaimed Arthur. 'She bought it in Lapis's shop, and that fellow whom you saw is no more the person you took him to be than I am. As for the talk about Lord Ellrington, I doubt not it is a scandalous lie, and so I'll make her confess before the day is at an end.'

He then rang the bell and ordered three or four of the servants to go immediately to Harley Street and take Miss Foxley and whomever they might find with her into custody. They soon returned, accompanied by the governess and her male accomplice, whom my father and brother instantly recognized as Edward Percy, the well-known scamp and oldest brother to the youth whose character he had assumed. He unblushingly declared that his only motive for joining in the fraud was to extort a sum of money; and Miss Foxley, finding herself thus deserted by her assistant, confessed the falsity of all she had pretended and explained the mystery of the paper in the casket by saying, that such an agreement had really existed between the Ladies Hume and Percy, but had never been put in practice on account of their husbands' refusing to consent.

My father then told her that if she wished to escape punishment for her wickedness, she must instantly leave Africa for some distant country and never set foot on its shores again. 'I give you your choice', said the duke, 'between two evils—exile or the pillory. Choose that which you consider the least.'

She chose the former, and was accordingly shipped off the next day. As for Edward Percy, my father gave him ten sovereigns for his candid confession and dismissed him well satisfied.

'Do you forgive my involuntary disobedience now, Arthur?' asked the once more happy Marian, when all was settled.

A smile and a kiss answered her more satisfactorily than words. And thus ends my Tale of the Secret.

Introduction   As in the previous tale, the narrator is Lord Charles,
"Lily Hart"   although his presence is nowhere so marked as in the
                    satiric passages of "The Secret." The circumstances
arising in "Lily Hart" presumably occur some years before the events of
"The Secret." If we assume a more-or-less coherent conception of the
history of the Glasstown Confederacy developed by Charlotte and
Branwell, we can place "Lily Hart" in the context of the great civil war described by Branwell in "Letters from an Englishman."[1] The insurrection is
described as beginning on 16 March 1831, the narrator at the moment being in the company of the Marquis of Douro and Prince John of Fidena,
who rush immediately into the fray. It is in this first day of fighting, presumably, that Charlotte begins her domestic drama with the discovery of
the wounded Mr. Seymour, later revealed as Fidena. The rebellion was
fomented by Alexander Rogue, Branwell's creation who became the
Alexander Percy of "The Secret" and other narratives.

If we allow for minor discrepancies, Charlotte's tale meshes tidily with
Branwell's earlier war story. The false identities assumed by Fidena and
Douro are required for secrecy, for Verdopolis was for a brief spell occupied
by the rebels, who would no doubt have imprisoned or executed these two
captains of the government forces. During the two months of Seymour's
convalescence, the capital would have been retaken by the government,
and the year's interval during which Lily sinks into poverty would have
seen the great provincial Battle of Fidena, in which Rogue was finally
defeated by government forces under John of Fidena. From this victory, we
must then assume, he comes to claim his bride. Douro himself takes his
bride in this interval, as we know from Charlotte's "The Bridal,"[2] in which
the narrator places their nuptials shortly after the beginning of the Great
Rebellion. However, in "The Spell,"[3] a story that casts a problematical light
over all of her tales of Douro, Charlotte creates a twin brother for her hero,

---

1. T. J. Wise and J. A. Symington, eds., *The Miscellaneous Unpublished Writings of Charlotte and Patrick Branwell Brontë*, 8:96. See Appendix I. The Brontë children were doubtless much interested at this time in the debates preliminary to the Reform Bill of 1832.

2. Wise and Symington, 8:202.

3. Wise and Symington, 8:377; printed in facsimile; separate edition by G. E. McLean, *The Spell: An Extravaganza. An Unpublished Novel by Charlotte Brontë* (London, 1931). Citations are from this edition.

who at times acts in his stead: "My Lady of Fidena," he claims, "I was the acquaintance of Lily Hart and not Zamorna [i.e., Douro]."[4]

If Douro's identity is in this tale obscure, that of John of Fidena becomes more clear. He is erroneously identified as John Percy (thus Alexander Percy's son) in the first published version of "The Spell"; this mistake is repeated in the Shakespeare Head edition of Brontë juvenilia,[5] perhaps because in "A Peep into a Picture Book" his portrait follows those of Alexander Percy and Zenobia, and he is referred to as "the son of Alexander."[6] As the closing scene of "Lily Hart" makes clear, however, his father Alexander is really Alexander Sneaky, King of Sneachieland and one of The Twelve—the original set of named soldiers who founded the Glasstown Confederacy. The Maria Sneaky of "The Secret" is his sister, as is the Lady Edith of "Lily Hart," also referred to in "The Spell."[7] The child John Augustus Sneaky appears also in "A Peep into a Picture Book" and with Douro's son Ernest in "A Brace of Characters."[8]

More important, however, than fixing John of Fidena among his proper relations is recognizing him as an early study for another John, the religious idealist St. John Rivers of *Jane Eyre*. This tall, grave young man with the lofty forehead, piercing eyes, and powerful mind is marked by the same reserve, the same sense of exalted standards. The hints of character we find in this tale of Fidena's betrothal are made explicit in "A Peep into a Picture Book," where he is referred to as "the Royal Philosopher."

> How grave! what severe virtue! what deep, far-sought and well-treasured wisdom! what inflexible uprightness! Integrity that Death could not turn from the path of right; Firmness that would stoop to the block rather than yield one jot of its just, mature, righteous resolution; Truth from which the agonies of the wheel would be powerless to wring a word of equivocation; and to speak verity, Pride that could be no more thawed than the icebergs of Greenland. . . . the virtues pictured in his stately features seem of that high and holy order which almost exempt

---

4. *The Spell*, p. 142.

5. *The Spell*, p. xliv; Wise and Symington, 9:491.

6. Wise and Symington, 8:359.

7. *The Spell*, p. 143.

8. Wise and Symington, 8:361, 9:50. Ernest's mother was Helen Victorina (see note 7, "The Secret"). Ernest, not to be confused with Marian's child, Julius, was later murdered in Mina Laury's arms by Douro's enemies.

their possessor from sympathy with mankind. Thoughts of martyrs and patriots, and zealous but stern prophets . . . recur to our minds.[9]

And when we observe that in "Lily Hart" the situations of Jane and Rivers are simply reversed—he the mysterious stranger in distress, she the ministering samaritan—we get some sense of the long preparation out of which *Jane Eyre* grew.

Finally, the two tales in this manuscript come together when we learn— again from "A Peep into a Picture Book"—that John of Fidena was Marian Hume's most trusted and most loyal friend. Often, we are told, she sat at his feet in conversation with him and his wife Lily; and in the dark days when she languished from Douro's neglect, he tended her faithfully until her death.

> On quitting the bedside, as he hung over his adopted sister for the last time, a single large tear, the only one anguish, bodily or mental, ever wrung from the exalted soul of the Christian philosopher, dropped on the little worn hand he held in his; and he muttered half aloud: "Would to God I had possessed this treasure; it should not thus have been thrown away."[10]

This intersection, however, merely closes one orbit in the complex cycle of tales that occupied Charlotte Brontë in her formative years. The reconstruction by now is substantial; but there are fragments yet to be retrieved, which, like these, once comprised the virtual universe that was the daily realm of her imaginative life.

---

9. Wise and Symington, 8:358–59.
10. Wise and Symington, 8:360.

It was on the evening of the memorable sixteenth of March, the day of the great insurrection, that Mrs. Hart, a respectable widow-lady, and her daughter Lily sat by the parlour fireside of their quiet and modest mansion, situated in one of the remote suburbs of Verdopolis. They had passed the day in a state of the most intense and feverish anxiety, hourly expecting that the flames of war, which were raging with such violence in other parts of the city, would spread to the obscure quarter in which they dwelt. Happily, however, about three o'clock P.M. the incessant thunder of distant artillery, which till then they had heard pealing from the far-off eastern division, began to die away. The cloud of smoke which hung so gloomily between earth and heaven waxed less dense, the tumultuous roar of battle grew fainter, and intelligence soon arrived that the rebellion had at length been completely put down by Government.

Hours elapsed before the two terrified females could free themselves from the flutter of excitement in which they had been kept all day. But when night fell down and all continued quiet, when several fresh messengers confirmed the good news, and when many of those who had been engaged in the combat, returning to their homes, declared that the army of rebels was utterly cut off, they began to feel themselves reassured, and after bolting the doors and fastening the windows of the house, ventured for the first time since morning to partake of a slight meal, which Bessie, their only servant, had managed, though half dead with fear, to prepare. When it was concluded both drew near to the fire. As yet, they felt too unsettled to engage in their usual occupations of reading or sewing, but sat talking over the fearful events of the day and conjecturing the probable consequences of this unsuccessful attempt against good government. While they were thus employed, Lily suddenly stopped short in the midst of a sentence she was uttering:

'Listen, Mama', said she. 'Do you not hear a noise in the garden?'

Her mother listened. 'I do', she replied. 'It sounds like the moan of someone in pain; perhaps it may proceed from some poor wounded creature, and if so, it is our duty to assist him.'

With these words, she stepped to a little glass door which opened into the garden. Lily followed her mother. It was a clear and still night; the moon and stars were shining most brilliantly in a perfectly unclouded heaven, and their descending beams revealed the form of a human being stretched on the grass near a little wicket which was open. Mrs. Hart called to the prostrate figure, but received no answer. She then went up to him and took his hand. It was very cold; he had ceased moaning and now lay motionless.

'I fear he is dead', said the benevolent lady, in a tone of compassion, 'but hasten, Lily, and tell Bessie to run instantly for the nearest surgeon.'

'I know something of the art of surgery', said a voice close at hand, while a tall figure entered by the open wicket. 'And if my skill would be of any use, it is at your service, madam.'

'Who are you, sir?' asked she, in some alarm at this sudden intrusion.

'An officer in the Grand Army of Verdopolis, madam, and one whom no individual of the fair sex needs to fear.'

Encouraged by the soft and gentle accent in which the stranger spoke, she expressed her gratitude for his timely offer of assistance; and soon the wounded man was, with the additional aid of Bessie, conveyed into the snug little parlour and safely deposited on a sofa. As the candle-light fell on his pallid features, the officer uttered an exclamation of surpise.

'I know this person', said he; 'he is my dearest friend. I trust to God he yet lives. If not, Africa has this day sustained a great loss.'

He then hastened to revive him by means of stimulants and cordial waters, which Mrs. Hart liberally supplied. Gradually he returned to life, and on opening his eyes, stared wildly round and would have spoken, but his military medical attendant strictly forbade him to utter a word. On examination, his wound was found to consist in a bayonet stab in the right side; it was not deep, and most fortunately the vital parts remained uninjured.

'By what name shall I call your friend, sir?' asked Mrs. Hart, when the wound was staunched and bandaged and the poor sufferer put to bed.

'Mr. Seymour', replied the officer, after a moment's consideration. 'And my name is Colonel Percival. If I could venture to urge so bold a request, madam, I should wish him to remain here till he is completely cured. I will be your guarantee for the reimbursement of such expenses as you may incur on his account.'

Mrs. Hart assured him of her perfect willingness to permit the stranger's sojourn; and then, after promising to call again next morning, Colonel Percival took his leave.

'What a handsome man that officer is', said Lily Hart when he was gone. 'I never saw such dark and sparkling eyes or such a magnificent form and face. But he looks very young to be a colonel.'

'He does, my dear', replied her mother. 'Most probably, however, he is a scion of some noble family. At least, I should conjecture so from his lofty and patrician appearance; and they, you know, obtain preferment early.'

Days and weeks passed away, and Mr. Seymour recovered rapidly under the treatment of his friend, who attended him with the most assiduous and constant care. The invalid's manners at first were not very prepossessing, in the opinion of his kind hostesses. He appeared cold and distant, and seemed to take all the attentions bestowed upon him as his right; but upon longer acquaintance, this chilly reserve thawed almost entirely away. As his wound healed, he became more agreeable; and when, at length, he was able to leave his bedroom and sit in the armchair by the little parlour-hearth, Lily wondered how she could ever have thought him either a plain or a proud man.

In person he was very tall, and so erect as to appear at times rather stiff and formal. His features were regularly formed, his forehead lofty and open, his eyes of a dark grey colour, deep-set and piercing. A general air of dignified gravity pervaded his whole countenance and, notwithstanding his youth, for he did not appear to be above twenty-five or six years of age, became him extremely well. He never laughed, but the contrast of his usual sobriety imparted an uncommon graciousness to his smile; but notwithstanding all this, his disposition was evidently turned to a fondness for domestic life and female society. He would sit in a rustic seat in the garden, when he was able, weaving a garland of roses for the head of Lily or the neck of her favourite lap-dog. He constructed a pretty moss house and adorned it with shells and pebbles. At times, though not often, he would accompany Miss Hart's guitar with his powerful yet melodious voice; and regularly every morning, he gave her lessons in the Italian language, in which he appeared to be a proficient and which she was studying. Then in the evenings, when the curtains were let down and the fire burned bright, while the ladies sat at their needlework, Mr. Seymour would read to them from some standard author, commenting on remarkable passages as he went on and illustrating such as were obscure, in language so lucid, so unassuming, and at times so eloquent, as to give them a most exalted idea of his understanding. When he became earnest in conversation, which he often did if the subject interested him, his countenance grew very animated, his eyes sparkled, and his words flowed forth with freedom, energy, and even brilliancy.

Often when he was thus awakened, Lily would drop her work and gaze on him earnestly; and then, when the tide of inspired feeling gradually ebbed, and he returned to his customary calm and stately demeanour, she would reassume it with an involuntary sigh. Mrs. Hart marked this and many other little indications of her daughter's [growing] regard for their guest. When Mr. Seymour spoke, Lily was all rapt and earnest attention; when he was unusually grave, a sympathizing sadness appeared on her face. If the slightest complaint of returning pain or weakness escaped him, she trembled lest he should relapse; and if a lighter tread or a gayer strain of conversation proclaimed improving health and spirits, her joy knew no bounds. All these tokens of incipient affection were noticed by the careful mother and occasioned her many an hour of anxious meditation; for though she could easily discern the state of her daughter's mind, yet that of the stranger defied her penetration. He was so sedate, so guarded, possessed such complete command over himself, that it was utterly impossible to read his thoughts in his countenance.

True, Lily was handsome enough to attract the attention of any man; and so my readers would have thought had they seen her. She was about eighteen years old, rather above than under the middle size, elegantly formed, with gracefully rounded limbs and small fairylike face and hands. Her complexion was of a rich and sunny tone of colouring. Dark, bright eyes, softened by long, silken lashes, diffused a most fascinating expression over her sweet face, and harmonized well with the wild black curls which waved in such luxuriant clusters over her glowing vermilion cheeks. To these attractions were added a charming simplicity of dress and manner, all the refined accomplishments of a polite education, and the more solid advantages of a useful one. Yet this lovely creature failed to excite any emotion in the, in this respect, almost stoical Mr. Seymour, beyond what was indicated by an occasional fixed gaze, which was instantly withdrawn and compensated for by an additional degree of gravity and restraint.

In the space of two months he was, by dint of good nursing, restored to perfect health; but yet he did not seem willing to depart. One morning, while they were sitting at breakfast, Colonel Percival happened to call. After a little desultory conversation, he began to urge on his friend the necessity of returning to his family, who, he said, were beginning to be very anxious about him. Mr. Seymour made no answer to his arguments, but appeared very loath to acknowledge their justice.

At length, the colonel said laughingly, 'Well, if you still refuse to quit your quarters, I shall begin to think someone has cast a spell round you. Perhaps my fair Lily here could furnish me with the name of the enchantress, if she would.'

A deep blush crimsoned the young philosopher's brow; he started up directly and exclaimed, 'I will go this instant, I will quit this peaceful retreat without delay. Mrs. Hart, allow me to offer you a very slight compensation for your unwearied kindness and attention towards me.'

So saying, he tendered her a banknote of two hundred pounds. This, however, his disinterested hostess most promptly refused. In vain he implored her to accept it: she would not, and in the end he was compelled to return it to his pocket-book. Then, turning to Lily, he took her hand, pressed it gently, slipped off a valuable diamond ring which decorated his little finger, placed it on hers, and with a faint, mournful farewell, abruptly left the house. Colonel Percival looked after him a moment with a significant smile, bowed gracefully to both the ladies and wished them a good morning, and departed.

A year elapsed, and during that little space of time poor Lily saw many and mighty changes. She had wept the loss of a loved and loving mother, whom a grave illness had in seven days' time carried to her grave; she had been left destitute by the failure of a banker in whose hands the whole of her small though competent fortune was lodged; and she had been forced to leave the house where she was born and brought up, and now resided in an humble dwelling containing only two apartments, where she endeavoured to support herself by manufacturing and selling ornamental articles such as screens, racks, [etc.]. All day long she sat engaged in the production of the most beautiful and elegant forms, yet her utmost diligence could only procure her the means of a very scanty subsistence. In the meantime, [several words illegible] with grief for her dear parent's death and another deep-seated and hopeless sorrow greatly impaired her health. She grew thin and pale; her step lost its elasticity, her eye its lustre, her cheek its bloom; and in short she faded to the mere shadow of her former self.

One evening, after toiling ten weary hours over scraps of cardboard and shreds of gilt paper, sick at heart with her thankless labour, she rose, and wrapping herself in a large mantle, left her house to seek relaxation in a short walk. Grateful was the freshness of the soft balmy summer's evening wind as it kissed her wasted cheek and played among her black, unbraided ringlets. The golden glory of a fast-westering sun lay on the distant harbour, brightened its busy shores, and lit up with a warm glow the rocklike structure which soars from the centre of magnificent Verdopolis. Unconscious whither her way tended, she paced slowly on, gazing now at the dazzling west, now at the far-off hills which shone dimly visible in the excess of radiance which suffused them, and now at the dark blue waters of the seemingly waveless sea. Such an assemblage of lovely objects quickly calmed her griefs and excited in her mind a train of soothing meditations.

Ere long she was roused from her delicious reverie by a hum of human voices and a tread of passing footsteps, which warned her that she had left her own quiet quarter of the city and was entering upon a busier [illegible]. She looked up and saw that she was in the wide and splendid street called Ebor Terrace. Heaven-aspiring palaces of the most superb and imposing architecture rose on each side, and seemed in their princely pride to frown away any poor plebian who might chance to fix his eye on them. This street, as my readers well know, is the Grand Corso of Verdopolis; and now, at the fashionable hour of sunset, it was crowded with hundreds of equestrians and pedestrians. Here groups of patrician beauties, lustrous in the fascination of bright eyes, lovely lips, beaming gems, and nodding plumes, glided stately by; and as they went, a soft perfume, and a sweet murmur of silver tones, lingered on the breeze behind them. There a stately chariot with six or eight fiery horses passed full speed like a rushing whirlwind, and everywhere the noble and the beautiful moved like beings of another sphere, seeming to disdain the ground on which they trod. As poor Lily looked round on the glittering forms of life and splendour, not one of whom would condescend to cast a look or waste a thought on her, she felt a sensation of utter loneliness, and breathing a deep sigh, turned to depart.

While she was hastily retracing her steps, she chanced to glance upwards at one of the majestic edifices frowning above her and saw, seated at an open window and gazing pensively at the brilliant crowds beneath, the well-remembered form of Mr. Seymour. At this unexpected sight, a smothered exclamation of joyful surprise burst from Lily's lips and a radiant light sparkled in her dark eye. She stood transfixed for a moment; and while yet lost in wonder and delight, he raised his eyes and they fell on her. Blushing deeply, she hung down her head and covered her face with her hands; when she looked again the window was closed and the welcome vision departed.

'Cruel man', thought she, while a shower of unbidden tears gushed forth. 'He might have spoken one little word to me, were it only for the sake of my mother's kindness.'

The recollection of her mother determined Lily to visit the grave where her beloved ashes reposed, and with the tardy tread of sorrow she took the way to St. Michael's Cemetery. Twilight had quenched the glory of the setting sun in soft and silent shades ere she reached that huge wilderness of tombs, and a pale crescent moon was gilding the gloomy groves of gigantic cypress trees as she sat down near an upright headstone of grey marble, which stood close under the lofty southern wall. Utterly unbroken was the frozen hush which hung over that [city] of the dead. No step, no voice waked an echo among the silent tombs; but soon the cathedral clock tolled the hour of vespers, and then there came floating on the night air the swell of a solemn organ from the holy minster, which stood bathed in heavy moonbeams not far distant, and the sublime sound of a sacred song. As the chant died away, Lily took up the tune and sang mournfully the following stanzas:

> Dark is the mansion of the dead,
>   Dark, desolate, and still:
> Around it dwells a solemn dread,
>   Within a charnel chill.
>
> O Mother! does thy spirit rest
>   In fairer worlds than ours?
> 'Mid tranquil valleys ever-blest,
>   And ever-blooming bowers?
>
> I trust it doth, for thy pale clay
>   Hath found no fair abode,
> Shut from the happy light of day,
>   Pressed by the cold earth's load.
>
> Yet Mother! I would rest with thee
>   In thy long dreamless sleep.
> Though dread its mute solemnity,
>   All voiceless, still and deep.
>
> And I would rest my weary head
>   Upon thy lifeless breast,
> Nor feel one shuddering thrill of dread
>   At what my temples prest.
>
> Earth is a dreary void to me,
>   Heaven is a cloud of gloom.
> Then Mother! let me sleep with thee,
>   Safe in thy stilly tomb.

She ceased, and throwing herself on the grassy grave, wept and sobbed bitterly. When this paroxysm of grief subsided, she rose, and was preparing to leave the cemetery, when a tall and dark figure glided from an adjoining cypress grove and stood before her. Overcome with terror at this unexpected apparition, she shrieked aloud.

'Does Miss Hart fear him whose life she saved?' said a deep calm voice. Lily answered not, but seized with sudden faintness, sank on a stone which stood near. The stranger seated himself beside her and took her passive hand. 'Has my Lily forgotten the ungrateful Seymour?' he asked in soothing accents.

'No! Never! Never!' was her enthusiastic reply. 'Nor will I, till death separates me from all mental associations.'

'From what I have just heard', said he, 'you have lost your earthly protector and are now left desolate in the world.'

'I am', replied she briefly.

He paused a moment and then said, 'Lily, you have doubtless by this time concluded that I have lost all recollection of you and your [household], but it is not so. I have striven indeed to forget you, laboured night and day to erase the impress of your too-dear image from my mind. To this end, I have sought the drawing-room and the ballroom, in order to find some form of superior loveliness, some mind of higher excellence, than those which haunted me like a heavenly vision. But in vain: not one could I discover amongst all the fairest and noblest of the land to vie with my peerless, my lovely Lily. At length, unable any longer to live without you, I determined, despite of foolish prejudice and family pride, to seek out the poor widow's daughter and gain her consent to a private union. With this resolution, I went about six months since to your house in the eastern suburbs, but it was empty and none knew whither you were gone. Since that time I have sought you, but in vain, till this evening, when I was gazing at the [groups] in Ebor Terrace, my eye rested on the long-desired form. I immediately quitted the house where I was, watched what way you took, followed you hither. And now, Miss Hart, will you be my wife or not? Say yes and you make a fellow creature happy for life; say no and you pronounce the death-doom of one who never wronged you.'

After such an appeal, who could have uttered the cold and chilling negation? Lily could not: she saw at her feet the grave, the philosophical Mr. Seymour, he who seemed to have subdued all the turbulent passions which agitate other men; she beheld him changed for her sake into a mere mortal lover; she heard him declare that his life's happiness depended on her decision; and she murmured a faint and faltering 'yes!'

'Bless you, my dearest!' exclaimed he with energy, while he snatched her hand and pressed it passionately to his lips. 'Bless you for that little word! You are now mine and mine alone, and nothing save death shall divide us.' After a pause, he continued in his usual composed and deliberate manner. 'Circumstances, Miss Hart, which I cannot now explain to you render it imperative that our union should be strictly private. Do you agree to this?'

'I do', she replied, for having unconditionally yielded the grand point, she could not now hesitate about trifles.

'Meet me, then', proceeded Mr. Seymour, 'tomorrow night at this hour in this place.'

She consented, and after one long and fervent embrace they parted. Some of my readers will doubtless consider that this was an imprudent transaction on the part of Lily, but let them remember that she loved Mr. Seymour more than her life, that besides him there was not one creature on earth in whom she could centre her stock of warm affections, and that she was a young and inexperienced girl who had not yet completed her nineteenth year.

The whole of the next day Lily employed in making her bridal attire, and when it began to grow dark she dressed herself in it. It was a gown of a dark-coloured silk such as suited well with her complexion, ornamented here and there with small knots of pink ribbon. A larger bow of the same material bound up the rich jetty tresses which otherwise would have hung lower than her waist and made them form a natural coronet on the top of her head. Thus simply arrayed she looked most lovely; excitement had restored the bright rose to her cheek and the lustrous light to her eye. And when wrapped in her dark mantle she again passed over Ebor Terrace, there was none amongst all the hundreds there whose tread was so bounding and elastic as her own.

The crescent moon was again rising when she entered St. Michael's Cemetery. A gusty, hollow-toned wind waved the great arms of the cypress trees as they stood like swart giants rising darkly against the twilight sky, and the last swell of the vesper organ was dying in the domed cathedral. Solemn and mournful were the sights and sounds of that darkling hour, but her buoyant spirits resisted the gloomy impression they were calculated to make, and full of happy anticipation she sought her mother's tomb. Her heart bounded as she saw a tall figure standing beside it, but on drawing nearer she perceived that it was not her lover but a military officer dressed in uniform; his sword and steel-clasped belt sparkled in the moonlight, and as he paced slowly to and fro with measured step he hummed the fragment of a merry march. Filled with dismay, she was about to retreat, when he suddenly raised his head and exclaimed, 'Is that you, Miss Hart?'

In the pronunciation of these words, Lily instantly recognized the deep melody of Colonel Percival's peculiarly fascinating voice, and the stranger's face being now turned to the light, she likewise knew the statuelike and noble beauty of his features. Now Lily had always admired the colonel because he was a handsome and graceful man, but she feared him likewise on account of a certain lofty imperiousness in his manner and in the expression of his bright and bold, dark eyes. His behaviour to her mother and herself had ever been perfectly kind and gentle, but there was a certain air of condescension mixed with it which, whenever she conversed with him, used to impress her with an indescribable feeling of awe. It was, therefore, with considerable misgiving and in a very timid tone that she answered his question in the affirmative.

'Do not be afraid, fair Lily', said he encouragingly. 'I am here on behalf of my friend, Mr. Seymour, who was prevented from coming himself to meet you by urgent business, any neglect of which would have excited inquiry and perhaps discovery, in which case the happiness he has so much at heart would infallibly have been snatched away from him at the moment of its completion. I hope you will not refuse to allow me to act as his substitute.'

Lily had gone too far to retreat, and she was therefore reluctantly compelled to accept the gay young officer as a conductor. When she had signified that she was ready to follow him, he uttered a shrill whistle, and immediately a splendid carriage dashed through the open gates of the cemetery. Having assisted her to enter it and placed himself by her side, he gave the word of departure, and off they rolled with the [celerity] of lightning.

The carriage blinds being down, Lily could not discern which way they went, but after an hour's rapid driving the vehicle suddenly drew up and Colonel Percival informed her that she must now alight. On getting out she saw before her the pillared entrance of a vast park. A footman unfolded the gates, and her guide, drawing her arm through his, proceeded to follow the carriage road till they came in sight of a most extensive and magnificent mansion, or rather palace, whose white marble columns and turrets were all gleaming with softest radiance in the tranquil moonbeams. He then turned, crossed an angle of the park and, opening a small arched door which was formed in a lofty wall by which this portion of the grounds was bounded, they entered a large garden. After threading their way through long [illegible] dark alleys through whose bowery arches scarcely a ray of light found ingress, and crossing open parterres where the closed and drooping blossoms and variegated green leaves were all wet and glittering with the tears of night, they at length reached a small chapel or oratory situated in the midst of a great wilderness of tall and fragrant flowering shrubs.

'Now,' whispered the colonel as they passed under the fretted porch and up the long echoing aisle, 'Now, fair Lily, I have discharged my trust and shall yield you to better hands.'

'And you have discharged it well', said the voice of Mr. Seymour, issuing from a neighbouring aisle. 'Adrian, I thank you, but do not depart till you have seen the indissoluble knot tied.'

He consented to remain in order to witness their union, and all three proceeded towards the altar, where a clergyman of a remarkably grave and venerable aspect stood ready in gown and cassock. In another quarter of an hour Lily Hart had changed her name and pledged her faith for life.

When the marriage ceremony was over, Percival took his friend's hand, warmly wished him joy, bade him farewell, and, after respectfully saluting the bride, departed.

'Now, my own dear Lily,' said Mr. Seymour, turning to his wife, 'we must leave Verdopolis without delay, if you do not already feel too much fatigued.'

Lily assured him that she was not at all tired, and leaving the chapel they returned to the park gate, where the carriage still awaited their arrival.

All night long their journey continued, and at last, just about sunrise, Mr. Seymour lifted one of the carriage blinds and bade his wife look out. She did so, and her eye beheld one of the fairest and most fertile scenes imagination can conceive. Emerald-green meadows stretched on every side, spotted here and there with tall, spreading forest trees and watered by a broad and placid river on whose banks, facing the east and bathed in the rosy light of early day, there appeared a small and elegant villa surrounded by a lawn and gardens and backed by a grove of tall young elm trees, whose branches, as they were shaken by the sweet morning wind, let fall a shower of dew on the clustering vines and roses which clung to its roof and sides.

'What a lovely place', said Lily. 'I should like to live there.'

'Your wish is granted, my love,' replied her husband, 'for that is your destined place of abode.'

And for three years Lily dwelt in this peaceful little paradise, in the midst of as perfect happiness as it is possible for mortal man or woman to enjoy. Surrounded by all the elegancies and comforts of life, blessed ere long by a beautiful and healthy boy, cherished by an affectionate and tender husband whose mild philosophical manners and calm, deep attachment never lost either their charm or their strength, who could be happy if she was not?

Yet there were one or two little circumstances which somewhat disturbed her felicity. In the first place, the mystery of their clandestine marriage still remained unsolved. She did not yet properly know who her husband was; she had never seen one member of his family or even heard him mention them. His anxiety to keep her in perfect seclusion was evident; he never once permitted her to visit Verdopolis, and no guest with the exception of Colonel Percival was ever allowed to enter Elm Grove Villa. In the second place, she was often for weeks together deprived of Mr. Seymour's own society. He seldom upon an aggregate spent more than the fourth part of the year with her, the rest being devoted to important business in the city. It is true, the brevity and fewness of his visits rendered them more delightful, but notwithstanding this, she could not help occasionally expressing a wish that she might see more of one so justly dear to her.

One evening at the commencement of the fourth year of her marriage, she, her husband, and Colonel Percival (whom Lily had learned [to] regard not only without fear but with feelings of the warmest and purest friendship) were all assembled in the villa drawing-room. It was a wild and tempestuous night. Torrents of rain dashed incessantly against the windows; a gusty wind swept in fierce but wailing howls through the crashing elm grove; and every now and then its melancholy voice was mingled with the dull muttering of distant thunder. This war of elements without the villa, however, seemed only to increase the cheerfulness of the party within. Lily, seated at her harp, was uttering tones melodious enough, one would have thought, to have charmed the wildest storm that ever rushed with blast and thunder through the midnight heavens. Her husband bent over her, listening in rapt attention to the sweetness of her voice and harp. As for Colonel Percival, he was busily engaged with his pet, little Augustus Seymour, now tossing him in his arms, now dancing before his dazzled eyes a glittering watch and chain, and then again teaching him how to handle and cock a small pistol which he loaded with powder and discharged once or twice, at which the bold, spirited child, instead of being terrified, clapped his hands and chuckled with delight at every explosion.

'Colonel,' said Lily, rising when she had ceased her song and advancing towards him with a smile, 'you will spoil my child by your too-great indulgence. Already he is getting as willful and unmanageable as— as—'

'As myself, madam, you would say', interrupted the colonel, laughing. 'Be it so, I have no desire to see him otherwise. If he could unite a little of my impetuosity with his father's wisdom, he would be perfect, you know.'

She was going to reply in the same half-playful, half-serious strain, when a tremendous peal of thunder burst just over their heads.

'The storm increases', observed Mr. Seymour. 'How dreadful must be the situation of those who are exposed to its fury.'

He had scarcely uttered these words when the sound of approaching carriage wheels, followed by a violent ringing of the door-bell and a correspondingly vigorous agitation of the knocker, proclaimed that there were persons without who suffered even now the pitiless drenching of the tempest. Directly after, a servant opened the door and announced that a gentleman and two ladies had arrived in an open chariot and requested shelter till the storm should pass over.

'Show them into the dining-room', said Mr. Seymour.

'The fire is gone out in that room, sir', replied the servant, 'and they are dripping wet.'

'Well, then, bring them here. I suppose, Adrian (looking toward the colonel), they are not persons who know anything of us, so it does not much signify.'

Steps were now heard on the staircase, the door was again flung open, and there entered first a tall, perpendicular, rigid-looking old gentleman of about sixty, with high bald forehead trimmed with a fringe of silver hair, aquiline nose, and very keen, piercing grey eyes. Then a lady who had passed the meridian of life but still retained in her benevolent countenance and mild blue eyes the remains of what had once been surpassing loveliness, and lastly a tall, slender, and beautiful girl. Both the ladies were enveloped in large dark velvet mantles lined with costly ermine; these rich garments were wet through and clung round them as if they had been flimsy taffeta.

The effect which the appearance of this imposing trio produced upon Percival and Seymour seemed very unaccountable to Lily. The former sprang up, exclaiming with an astonished smile, 'Lord bless me, the day of discovery is come at last, the hour when the secrets of all hearts shall be revealed. But never mind, John, stand it out boldly like a man. Flinch not, lie not, but make a clean bosom and take what shall come thereafter.'

Mr. Seymour did not seem greatly to need this advice. He had stood up and with folded arms and an air of cool determination had taken his station just opposite the door.

'What means all this, my lord Marquis?' asked the old gentleman, looking sternly at Colonel Percival. 'Why do I find you and my son here, and who is this woman?'

'That woman,' replied Seymour in a firm but respectful tone, 'that woman, my royal father, is my dear wife Lily, Marchioness of Fidena. I crowned her with my coronet three years since, and there by her side stands my son and your grandson, John Augustus Sneaky.'

The appearance of a thousand disembodied spirits could not have striken the royal party with more mute astonishment than did this simple piece of intelligence. At length, after gazing at his son silently for some minutes, the monarch Alexander spoke:

'Do not think to impose on me thus', he said. 'That presumptuous woman shall return immediately to her native obscurity, from which you have so wickedly raised her, unless you can produce the fullest proof of your marriage and unless that marriage was solemnized by the Chief Prelate, for no humbler priest can lawfully wed a prince of the blood.'

'I can bear witness to your majesty', replied Colonel Percival, or as we must now call him, the Marquis of Douro, for such he really was, 'that about this time three years since, John, Prince of Fidena, was united to Lily Hart by Gravey, the Metropolitan Archbishop himself, before the high altar of the private chapel situated in the gardens which surround your imperial palace on the banks of the Niger, I standing by and giving away the bride with my own hands.'

A dark and ominous flush covered Alexander's haughty brow when he heard this pronounced by the unabashed marquis in a tone of the most perfect and easy nonchalance. What he would have said or done I know not, but just as he was about to speak, the queen and her eldest daughter Lady Edith (my readers will have already recognized these exalted personages in the two females who accompanied him) flung themselves at his feet and implored him to forgive what could not now be undone and to receive once more to his paternal favour the son who till now had never offended him. Lily, trembling like an aspen leaf and pale as her floral namesake, joined her tears to their entreaties. Alexander, however, remained quite unmoved by their supplications and would probably have given free vent to the indignation which boiled within him, had not the Marquis of Douro stepped up to him and whispered in a low, emphatic tone:

'Monarch of the mountains, you may indeed cast this son away, but where will you turn to find another? Who shall be more worthy to inherit your crown and throne? Nowhere: therefore royalty must depart from your line and the sceptre pass into the hands of aliens.'

'You have spoken truth', replied the twelve* after a pause. 'Therefore, Prince John, I forgive you: but take notice it is not from the weakness of compassion, but merely because necessity compels me to it. Had I another son who was yet guiltless of any such daring act of disobedience, I would disown you, your wife, and child instantly and forever.'

Prince John made no answer to this speech of his royal father's; he only bowed low, and raising his kneeling wife said, with a pride almost equal to that of Alexander himself, 'Now, my Lily, you shall appear in the circles for which nature designed you, and if anyone dare breathe a word of scorn against you or yours, by heaven, that word shall be his last.'

On Monday last, the Marchioness of Fidena made her first public appearance in Verdopolis at a grand ball given on the occasion at Elimbos Palace, the residence of the king her father-in-law. I saw her and can safely state that Lily Hart, the widow's daughter, is worthy for grace and beauty to rank with the noblest born and fairest of Verdopolis.

---

* As used here, twelve is a title, roughly equivalent to a title such as 'apostle'. Alexander Sneaky was one of the original twelve toy soldiers, thus one of the founders of the Glasstown Confederacy. They were sometimes referred to collectively as The Twelves, hence the singular term used here.

Enlarged Facsimile

CHAPTER THE 1ST

A dead silence had reigned in the Home office of Verdopolis for three hours on the morning of a fine summer's day interrupted only by such sounds as the scraping of a penknife the dripping... [the remainder of the page is a densely written, heavily faded handwritten manuscript that is largely illegible]

She employed every art to draw away my brother's affections from the little unsophisticated girl who in her opinion knew not how to appreciate their value. Her efforts however were unsuccessful. They excited disgust instead of love & at length one afternoon when she... more than usually forward Arthur plainly though politely intimated that she was rather too ill & absurd to form a fit wife for him. This was sufficient to kindle all the bad passions in Miss Bird's mind she...

CHAPTER THE II.nd

When the marquis was gone he...

In the grove
Alone... the dark will see
Al...... while I am gazing
While... its ..... unceasefully
Through the dim gloaming

O these deep hollow tones
Sad thoughts inspire
They ...... like the thrilling .... moans
From ...... swept lyre

Echos from rock & cave
Silently dying
Answer the howling wave
Hark the winds sighing

Far in the silent sky
wandering ...... worlds quiver
Thus they shall beam on high
Changeless for ever

But yon ...... moon
Silvers the billow
Ocean will be my tomb
Sea-sand my pillow

Then my unhallowed name
None shall remember
Gone like the ...... flame
Quenched like the ember

94

CHAPTER THE III.

97

CHAPTER THE IV.th

98

LILY HART

hour of vespers & then there came floating on the night-air, swell of a solemn organ from the holy minster which stood bathed in heavy moonbeams not far distant & the sublime sound of a sacred song, as the chant died away Lily took up the theme & sang mournfully the following stanzas.

Dark is the mansion of the dead
　Dark desolate and still
Around it dwells a solemn dread
　Within a cloister'd chill

O mother! does thy spirit rest
　In fairer worlds than ours?
'Mid tranquil valleys ever blest
　And ever blooming bowers?

I trust it doth, for thy pale clay
　Hath found no fair abode
Shut from the happy light of day
　Pressed by the cold earth's load

Yet mother! I would rest with thee
　In thy long dreamless sleep
Though I read its mute solemnity
　All voiceless, still & deep

And I would rest my weary head
　Upon thy lifeless breast
Nor feel one shuddering thrill of dread
　At what my temples prest

Earth is a dreary void to me
　Heaven is a cloud of gloom
Then ... let me sleep with thee
　Safe in thy stilly tomb

She ceased &...

when the secrets of all hearts shall be revealed, but never mind John. stood it out boldly like a man...

Forsyth. 33   Charlotte Brontë

THE SECRET
AND
Lily Hart.　Two Tales

by Lord
Charles
Wellesley
Verdopolis

THE . . . SECRET

CHAPTER THE Ist

A dead silence had reigned in the Home office of Verdopolis for three hours on the morning of a fine summer's day interupted only by such sounds as the scraping of a penknife the
dropping of a ruler an occasional cough or whisper & now & then some brief mandate uttered by
the noble ₍first₎ secretary in his commanding tones. at length that sublime personage after completing
some score or so of despatches addressing a small slightly built young gentleman who occupied
the chief situation among the clerks said "Mr Ryhmer will you be good enough to tell me what
'clock it is" "Certainly my lord" was the prompt reply as springing from his seat the ready underling instead of consulting his watch like other people hastened to the window in order to mark
the sun's situation, having made his observations he answered 'tis twelve precisely my lord"
"Very well" said the marquis "you may all give up then & see that all your desks are locked & that
not a scrap of paper is left to litter the office, Mr Rhymer I shall expect you to take care that
my directions are fulfilled". So saying he assumed his hat & gloves & with ᵃ stately ~~step~~ ₍tread₎ was ap~~proa~~
proaching the vestibule when a slight bustle & whispering among the clerks arrested his steps
What is the matter asked he turning round "I hope these are not sounds of contention I hear"
"No" said a broad carrotty locked young man of a most pugnacious aspect "but—but, your lordship has forgotten that—that—" "That what" asked the marquis rather impatiently "Oh! merely
that this afternoon is a half-holiday, and—and" "I understand" replied his superior smiling "you
need not task your modesty with further explanation. Flannagan the truth is I suppose you
want your usual largess. I am obliged to you for reminding me, will that do" he continued as
~~take~~ opening his pocket-book he took out a twenty-pound bank bill & laid it on the nearest desk
My lord you are too generous" Flannagan began but the chief secretary laughingly laid his
gloved hand on his lips & with a condescending nod to the other clerks sprang down the steps of
the portico & strode hastily away in order to escape the noisy expression of gratitude which now
hailed his liberality. On the opposite side of the long & wide street to that on which the splendid
Home office stands, rises the no less splendid [Persian] office Colonial office. just as Arthur mar-

quis of Douro left the former structure Edward Stanley Sydney departed from the latter, they
met in the centre of the street, Well Ned" said my brother as they shook hands, how are you
to day I should think this bright sun & sky ought to enliven you if anything can," "Why my dear
Douro" replied Mr Sydney with a faint smile, "such lovely & genial weather may & I have no doubt
does elevate the spirits of the free & healthy, but for me whose mind & body are a continual prey
to all the heaviest cares of public & private life it signifies little whether sun cheer or rain damp
the atmosphere, "Fudge," replied Arthur his features at the same time assuming that disagree
able expression which my landlord denominates by the term scorney "Now don't begin to bore
me Ned with trash of that description I'm tired of it, quite, pray have you recollected that to
day is a half-holiday in all departments of the Treasury? "Yes & the circumstance has cost me
some money, these silly old customs ought to be abolished in my opinion, they are ruinous"
"Why what have you given the poor fellows?" "Two sovereigns" an emphatic hem formed Arthur's reply to this communication. They had now entered Hotel-Street & were proceeding in
silence past the line of magnificent shops which it contains, when the sound of wheels was
heard behind them & a smooth rolling chariot dashed up & stopped just where they stood
One of the window glasses now fell a white hand was put out & beckoned them to draw near
while a silvery voice said "Mr Sydney, marquis of Douro come hither a moment," both the gentlemen obeyed the summons with alacrity, Sydney with reluctance, What are your commands
fair ladies" said the former ˄ to the inmates of the carriage who were Lady Julia Sydney and Lady Maria Sneaky. "Our commands are principally for your companion my lord not for you" replied the daughter of Alexander the first, now Mr Sydney she continued smiling on the senator
you must promise not to be disobedient" Let me first know what I am required to perform
was the cautious answer accompanied by a fearful glance at the shops around. "Nothing of
much consequence Edward" said his wife "but I hope you'll not refuse to oblige me this once
love I only want a few guineas to make out the price of a pair of earings I have just seen in
Mr Lapis's Shop." Not a bit of it" answered he "Not a farthing will I give you It is scarce three
weeks since you received your quarter's allowance & if that is done already you may suffer for it
with this decisive reply he instinctively thrust his hands into his breeches pockets & marched
off with a hurried step. "Stingy little monkey" exclaimed Lady Julia sinking back in the carriage
seat while the bright flush of anger & disappointment crimsoned her fair cheek "this is the
way he always treats me but I'll make him suffer for it." Do no discompose yourself so much
my dear" said her companion "my purse is at your service if you will accept it." "I am sensible
of your goodness Maria, but of course I shall not take advantage of it, no no I can do without the
earings It is only a fancy though [illegible] I would rather have them" "My pretty cousin
observed the marquis who till now had remained a quiet though much amused spectator of
the whole scene "you are certainly one of the most extravagant young ladies I know, but since
your mind is so why what on earth can you possibly want with those trinkets to my knowledge you have at least a dozen different sorts of ear ornaments," "That is true but then these

are quite of another kind, they are so pretty & unique that I could not help whishing for
them," "Well since your heart is so much set upon the baubles I will see whether my purse
~~will~~ can compass their price if you will allow me to ~~compass~~ accompany you to Mr Lapis's." O! thank you
Arthur you are very kind" said Lady Julia & both the ladies quickly made room for him as he
sprang in & seated himself between them. "I think" said Maria Sneaky who has a touch of
the romp about her "I think when I marry I'll have just such a husband as you my lord marquis "one who won't deny me a pretty toy when I have a desire to possess it" Will you, said Arthur, "I really think the Turks are more sensible people than ourselves" In a few minutes
they reached the Jeweler's Shop. Mr Lapis received them with an obsequious bow & proceeded to
display his glittering stores. the pendants which had so fascinated lady Julia were in the form of
two brilliant little hummingbirds ~~the [illegible]~~ whose jewelled plumage equalled if not surpassed the
bright hues of nature, whilst she was completing her purchase A customer of a different
calibre entered, this was a tall woman ~~dressed~~ attired in a rather faded silk dress. a large bonnet & a
double veil of black lace which as she lifted it on entering the shop discovered a countenance
which apparently ~~[illegible]~~ had witnessed the vicissitudes of between thirty & forty summers
her features might or might not have been handsome in youth, though they certainly
exhibited slight traces of beauty now, on the contrary a sharp nose, thin blue lips & flat eyebrows formed an assemblage of rather repulsive lineaments even when aided by highly
rouged cheeks & profusely frizzed dark locks. One would have thought that such a person [illegible]
as I have described would have attracted but little attention from a young and gay nobleman like my brother he however fixed his ~~keen~~ piercing [illegible] eye upon her the moment
she made her appearance, his gaze nevertheless did ~~[illegible]~~ not indicate ~~[illegible]~~ admiration rather ~~expressed~~ but curiosity & contempt, a keenly inquisitive expression mingled with one of scorn filled his countenance while
he watched her. With a slow & stiff movement she approached the counter and addressing a shopman desired to look at some rings. he instantly lifted the glass case & exposed to her view several hundreds of the articles she wanted. Deliberately the lady examined them all but not one would
suit, Diamonds, rubys, pearls, emeralds, topaz, [etc.] were each in their turn inspected & rejected. [her]
At length the shopman who was a little out of patience at her extreme fastidiousness of choice inquired
what description of ring she could possibly want since the first jewellers depot in Verdopolis did not
contain it. "The ring I am in quest of" replied she "should be very small of plain gold with a chrystal
stone, containing a little braided chestnut-couloured hair & this name (taking a scrap of paper from
her reticule) engraven on the inside." Well madam" answered he "we certainly have not just
such an article as that in the shop at present but we could very easily make one for you"
could you finish it today?" asked she "Yes" "then do so I will call for it this evening at nine o'clock"
with these words she turned to leave the shop. her eyes as she lifted them from the counter
fell on the marquis & met his scrutinizing glance, for a moment she seemed to quail under
~~[illegible]~~ its influence but presently recovering herself dropped him a low curtsey which was returned
by a very slight & haughty bow & sailed into the street. "Who is that ~~[odious]~~ odd looking woman" asked

Lady Julia as she drew on her gloves after having finally completed her tedious bargain, the marquis made no answer, but Maria Sneaky said with an arch look "Some ci-devant chère amie of ~~the~~ Douro's, I suppose or perhaps a lady who will hereafter partake with me the benefit of a [illegible] matrimonial dispensation" "Is it so? Arthur?" inquired his cousin "Nay Julia I shall not tell you, you may draw your own inferences from the circumstances of the case. When he had assisted the ladies to their chariot, received his due tribute of parting smiles & thanks & beheld the brilliant equipage roll merrily off my brother turned down Hotel Street & directed his steps towards Victoria Square. A thoughtful & somewhat moody cloud [~~illegible~~] darkened his brow as he entered Wellesley house ascended the grand staircase & proceeded through a succession of passages & chambers to the marchioness's appartment. On opening the door & drawing aside the green damask curtain which hung within he found her seated alone at a table & engaged in finishing a pencil sketch. She raised her head as he approached & welcomed him with a smile whose sweetness was more eloquent than words. "Well Marian" said he bending over her to look at the drawing "What is this you are about" "Only a little landscape my lord which I sketched in the valley yesterday" "It is really very pretty & most charmingly pencilled I think I remember the view, Is it not from the gateway of York Villa". Yes Arthur & I have introduced Mr Sydney in the fore-ground with a book in his hand." The marquis now sat down beside his wife & continued for sometime silently watching the progress of her pencil, at length he recommenced the conversation by saying Whom do you think I have seen in the city to-day Marian?" "I'm sure I don't know, perhaps [~~Theophilus~~ Julius] I desired Mina to take him out for an airing about half an hour since" "No you are far wrong in your guess". "Who then?" "no other than your old governess Miss Foxley." "At hearing this name the coulour faded from Marian's cheek, she paused in the midst of her employment & slowly raising her large blue eyes from the paper fixed them on Arthur with a look of deep alarm. he observed her agitation & the thoughtful aspect of his countenance darkened into something like displeasure as he continued "What Marian is not that inexplicable spell yet broken, I thought absence & kind treatment might do much, but it appears all my affection has not yet succeeded in erasing that impression which by some mysterious means Miss Foxley ~~has~~ contrived to make on your too sensitive mind" Tears now began to fill the marchioness's eyes & were dropping unheeded on her drawing as she answered in a subdued tone "do not be angry ~~with~~ Arthur." "I am not angry ~~with you~~ Marian" he replied "but can you deny that it was owing to that creature's cursed influence that you so long & steadfastly refused my hand, heart & coronet even when as you have often confessed your inclination was not averse to the offer & when as I could perceive a final rejection would have blasted your happiness for life. Is it not from that cause that those transient periods of melancholy arise with which you are even now oppressed" Marian made no answer he went on "How you at length summoned sufficient courage to throw off her shackles & consent to felicity I know not nor is my penetration sufficiently keen to divine, but it appears there are yet some lingering remains of her power. Come Marian dismiss this weakness, how can she hurt you whilst under my protection, make me your father confessor you cannot find one more indulgent & reveal all". Still there was no reply, the marquis now rose in anger "this is obstinacy Marian" he said "as well as weakness I shall leave you for the present to reflect on the consequences of a continuance in such folly but first let me warn you that I shall not suffer that woman to enter my house or ^permit you to have any communication with her [~~several words illegible~~] if I find my commands in this respect are disobeyed I shall consider our interest as thenceforth separate, it is no part of my plan to ~~suffer~~ ^allow the existence of a counteracting influence to my own in that heart & family where I ~~desire~~ ^ought to reign paramount" With these words he closed the door & in a few minutes the echo of his retreating footsteps died away along the distant corridor. It may perhaps be necessary to give my reader a more particular account of Miss Foxley before I proceed with my narrative, this I shall do in as few words as possible she was the only child of a respectable merchant who died insolvent leaving her an orphan at the age of ~~eighteen~~ twenty-one with no other fortune than her accomplishments which were numerous & her abilities which though not of the highest order were nevertheless of a kind well fitted to enable her to push her way through the world consisting chiefly in a capacity of discovering people's natural dispositions & adapting herself to them so as to worm a way into their good graces & a certain sharp-sighted shrewdness wherever her own interests were concerned. in early youth she was not devoid of personal graces but her beauty bore no proportion to her vanity & any wound in that quarter never healed [~~illegible~~] but continued to fester till revenge in some tangible shape was achieved on the offending person. On her father's death being unable to support her self in independence she entered the family of the late lady Hume in the situation of Companion & as such contrived so far to secure the confidence of that aimiable & unsuspicious woman that on the birth of Marian she was appointed Governess, for which office she was well qualified as far as talents & acquirements went. After lady Hume's death which took place when her daughter was fourteen years old, Miss Foxley still continued to reside at Sir Alexander's residence in Wellington's Land & was there when Arthur began to pay his addresses to her lovely young pupil. Unfortunately the Governess who had now numbered her thirty-fifth year was prompted by her unextinguishable vanity to imagine that she yet possessed charms potent enough to attract the admiration of a handsome & high-born [~~illegible~~] nobleman. Under the influence of this delusion she employed every art to draw away my brother's affections from the little unsophisticated girl who in her opinion knew not how to appreciate their value. her efforts however were unsuccessful they excited disgust instead of love & at length one afternoon when she ^had been more than usually forward ~~my~~ Arthur plainly though politely intimated that she was rather too old & obscure to form a fit wife for him. This was sufficient to kindle all the bad passions in Miss Foxley's mind she vowed mentally to make him regret his cold & scornful rejection & thenceforth set herself sedulously to work ^in order to prevent his union with her beautiful & youthful rival. The effect of her endeavours soon became but too apparent. For some time Marian ~~shunned~~ ^carefully avoided her noble lover, refused his hand shunned his attentions & so managed that Arthur marquis of Douro the proudest & haughtiest youth of Verdopolis was reduced to the condition of a pining, consumptive, love-sick young gentleman. Meantime it was universally believed in the city that the delay of his union with the daught[er] of Sir A Hume was owing to my father's opposition. ~~What~~ How great would have been the surprise of all ranks had it been known by whom the objection was really started. It was evident however that Miss Hume's perseverance in this course was not unattended with pain to herself, her wan looks attenuated form & tearful eyes soon proclaimed that there was a wasting worm within. Still however she constantly refused to listen to my brother's passionate professions & the triumph of Miss Foxley's intrigues was nearly completed when one day Arthur having resolved to make a last attempt & then give up in despair, arrived at Badey Hall to his astonishment he was at once shown into Marian's drawing room where he found her alone, what eloquent arguments he made use of to plead his cause, I know not, certain it is however that he was this time successful & three weeks after his lovely tyrant amidst smiles, tears, blushes pledged her troth to him at the high alter [St Michael's] Cathedral The first act of his authority as a husband was to comand the immediate dismissal of Miss Foxley who was consequently turned to the right about. he subsequently attempted to win from Marian an explanation of the causes which had so long delayed his happiness but on this subject she maintained a mysterious silence & he had for some time ceased to trouble her about it till the governess's reappearance brought it again most unpleasantly to his memory.

CHAPTER THE IInd

When the marquis was gone Marian with a deep sigh bent again over [illegible] her half-finished picture but now the pencil seemed to have lost its power or the hand which directed it its skill. instead of the flowing correct lines & soft shadows which she had before produced, tremulous wavering strokes & dark blotches mocked her unavailing efforts. at last she relinquished the attempt & after replacing her the [illegible] sketch in her portfolio & locking closing the ivory-box which contained her drawing materials, she drew towards her a harp which stood near. at first her slender, snowy fingers only extracted a few melancholy though sweet notes from the quivering strings but soon these unconnected sounds gave place to a melody simple yet exquisitely plaintive & ere long the according tones of her flutelike voice changed it to a delicious harmony while she sung the following little metrical fragment

on the shore of
Alone by the dark wild sea
Alone Silent whilst I am roaming
While sounds its waves voice mournfully
Through the dim gloaming

O those deep hollow tones
Sad thoughts inspire
They sound swell like the thrilling tones moans
From wind breeze-swept lyre

Echos from rock & cave
Solemly dying
Answer the howling wave
Mock the wind's sighing

110

Far in the silent sky
Wandering ~~stars~~ worlds quiver
Thus they shall beam on high
Changeless for ever

But ere another moon
Silvers the billow
Ocean will be my tomb
Sea-sand my pillow

Then my unhallowed name
None shall remember
Gone like the dying flame
Quenched like the ember

There were yet two verses of the fragment unsung when she was interrupted by a rap at the
door. "Come in" said the marchioness & Mina entered carrying a lovely infant. "Well my darling
^{exclaimed she} as with an assumed expression she rose & held out her arms to receive the pretty scion ^{of cheerfulness} "How are you
after your walk "the fresh air has brought a little coulour into his cheeks my lady" replied Mina relinquish
ing her charge. "I see it has & since that is the case you had better take him out daily for the future
Mina", _{Yes [I shall] my lady} replied the waiting maid seating herself at a small work-table & taking up a white robe
which she ^{had} previously been embroidering for her mistress. Marian for a few minutes continued talking to her little ^{Julius} ~~Theophilus~~ & endeavouring to amuse him with the coral & gold bell suspended round
his waist but soon sad thoughts seemed to come over her mind for she ceased to speak & sat gazing
on the child with eyes of mournful meaning. Mina who is a shrewd penetrating girl firmly attached
to the marchioness & high in her confidence presently perceived this depression of spirits & desirous
to learn the cause of it she broke silence by saying "I fear something has happened to vex my lord
"What makes you think so" asked Marian starting "because when I met him on the strand a little
while since he neither spoke to me nor lord ^{Julius} ~~Theophilus~~ as he always does if he is in a good temper
but past on & with a grave sorrowful look though the little darling cried to go to him" To these words
the marchioness made no reply. Mina resuming her work continued to trace the rich pattern in
silence. They continued thus employed for about half an hour when a second rap was heard at the
door. Mina rose to open it a footman stood without with a letter, "Who brought this William" asked
his lady after a hasty glance at the seal & direction, "A little boy my lady who said that it had been
given him by a woman in Harley-Street" "Is he gone?" "Yes ma'am" Very well William
that will do." Hurridly Marian broke the seal & ^{ran} ~~glanced~~ over the contents of the letter her
features whitened while she read & at the conclusion it dropped from her nerveless hand &
she would have fallen to the ground had not the ready Mina been in an instant at her side
Happily she did not faint on the contrary a few minutes restored the vanishing rose to her cheek &
lip. she then desired to be left alone "You may carry your work Mina into my dressing-room

said she." "& take ‸Julius T̶h̶e̶o̶p̶h̶i̶l̶u̶s̶ to his nurse let no one come here till I ring the bell I wish to be l̶e̶f̶t̶ ‸undisturbed [i̶l̶l̶e̶g̶i̶b̶l̶e̶] for a short time. Mina accordingly a̶c̶c̶o̶r̶d̶i̶n̶g̶l̶y̶ withdrew & it was midnight before she was again summoned to attend her lady. all the other servants had retired to rest an hour before & she alone remained in the deserted Hall anxiously awaiting the expected [i̶l̶l̶e̶g̶i̶b̶l̶e̶] sound at length just as she had formed the resolution to go uncalled f̶o̶r̶ Twelve o'clock struck & the wished for tinkle sounded. On opening the d̶o̶o̶r̶ sitting-room door she saw the marchioness placed ‸exactly j̶u̶s̶t̶ as she had left her in a chair near the hearth resting her head against the mantle-piece. There was no f̶i̶r̶e̶ candle in the appartment & in the grate the last feeble embers were just expiring "Will you not go up-stairs now my lady" asked Mina I have brought your bed-room lamp" "No Mina, not yet, but come in I want to speak to you." The waiting-maid closed the door & sat down in a chair which her mistress pointed out. Marian then continued "You know the marquis Mina as well as I do & that being almost perfect himself he cannot brook imperfection in others. his word & command have hitherto been my law to which I have always submitted myself with cheerfulness and pleasure. Tonight however I am going to set in direct opposition to his will, utter necessity must plead my excuse for such otherwise unpardonable disobedience but if he discovers it I am lost. Do you know where Harley-Street is Mina I must go there this night" "No my lady I do not but surely you do not intend to go alone" Yes I do" "That cannot be my lady you would be lost in the city, do let my father go with you he knows every street & lane of Verdopolis" "Is he in the house" "Yes my lord ordered him to sleep here every night" "Call him then" Mina left the room & in about ten minutes returned accompanied by her father. Ned halted at the door for a moment "Come in Edward said the marchioness in her sweet mild tone "I was only stripping my shoen my lady" said he "'cause they're not fit to walk on such a grand carpet as this" "O never mind that" replied she with a faint smile at his punctilious decorum "I am sorry to have called you from your bed Edward but I whished to learn from you what quarter of the city Harley-Street is situated in." "Harley-Street, why it's the same as they call Paradise-Street my lady cause there's a house in it that you would'nt like to pass by yourself at this time of night" "Should I not? then will you go with me" "That I will with all the pleasure in life." "Fetch my hat & cloak then Mina" "had you not better take mine my lady" asked the prudent fille de chambre." "yes on second thoughts that would certainly be the best." Mina again left the room & shortly came back with a plain straw hat & brown silk mantle. In these she attired her young mistress & then after lighting the fair o̶n̶e̶ adventurer & her guide down a private staircase to a street door of which she possessed the key returned to the servant's Hall & stretching herself on a chnintz sofa w̶h̶i̶c̶h̶ that ‸stood at the side of the still blazing hearth was soon buried in a profound sleep. The night was wild & stormy. vast billowy clouds from which a drizzling rain incessantly distilled rolled over the sky & at times as they parted their folds the serene moon was revealed shining far beyond them. A chill north wind mingled its moaning with that of the troubled sea whose howling waves might now be heard uttering their voice afar off. With a light step & beating heart Marian trod the wet, gloomy streets preceded by her trusty conductor. after passing through many wide squares & long broad streets.they entered a dark lane which would scarcely admit more than four persons abreast. on one side a line of lofty buildings arose. In the centre of which a sudden burst of moonlight discovered

112

a flight of steps surmounted by a portico. This is Harley Street my lady said Ned stopping & turning [illeg.]
around. Is it Edward" replied she in a low tone & then as if seized with a sudden agitation she sank on
the
steps before mentioned. scarcely had she sat their for five minutes when the sound of many footsteps [illegible] was heard approaching all was now again dark so that nothing could be distinguish
persons
ed but as the drew near Marian easily recognized several by their voices. "I think vice-president
we are late tonight" said one in a deep calm tone "Yes most worthy [illegible]" was the reply uttered
voice
in a [illegible] which struck chill dismay to the marchioness' heart & caused her instantly to take refuge
behind a sort of projecting pillar. "yes we are & I'll wager ten to one that Gordon proposes to fine us
for it." "Taken my lord marquis" exclaimed another. "Is that O'Connor?" asked the former speaker "Yes"
"Done then & I hope to fleece you well my most excellent knight of the mattock." here [illegible] the
door within the vestibule opened & a sudden glare of lamps streamed on the dense dark night
revealing the forms of about twenty or thirty gentlemen most of them tall handsome men

Pride in their port ~~these~~ defiance in their eye
These mighty lords of human-kind passed by

Tumultuously they sprang or rushed up the steps into a vast & magnificent hall blazing with
sunlike chandeliers which appeared above. Then the door closed [illegible] & night reassumed her sol-
rare
emn silent reign. "Those are [illegible] chaps" said Ned as he rejoined the terrified marchioness "If they
had seen you there would have been some'at to do only his lordship was there & that would have [illeg.]
checked them a bit I guess." "Let us proceed now Edward" said she "Which house are we to stop at my
lady" "The last in the street on the left hand" they soon reached it & Marian after directing Ned
to wait on the outside till she should return knocked timidly at the door. it was presently opened by
dingy
a dirty looking servant wench in a [illegible] lace cap & gaudy cotton gown. Is there not a lady of the name
of Miss Foxley lodging here" asked the marchioness. "Yes, ma'am & if you'll follow me I'll show you
her appartment, accordingly after carefully ~~fastin~~ fastening the door she led the way up a narrow
flight of stone steps & through a sort of lobby which was dimly lighted by a single lamp to an room
at the further end, entering first she announced that the lady was come "Indeed! said some one
within "Bring her here directly" & the visitor was ushered into a small chamber whose furniture con-
cane
sisted of a mahogany pembroke table, five or six [illegible]-bottomed chairs a scanty carpet, faded green
window curtains & a broken paper screen. a small but bright fire burnt in the grate & beside it a
tall female was seated in an arm chair. she rose as Marian entered & advanced to meet her saying "My lady marchioness how are you, I am surprised at your condescension in deigning to visit so obscure an individual as myself, pray be seated if ~~one of~~ these poor chair are not too mean to support a peeress of the
realm. Miss Foxley" replied the marchioness as she took the offered seat "I have run considerable risk
in complying with your request nor am I sure that my conduct in this respect is right, but my anxiety to learn the truth of what your letter hinted at induced me to disregard all other considerations
without delay
pray give me a more explicit account ~~now~~ "Why madam" returned the governess with a fiendlike smile "You are doubtless now a happy wife loving & beloved the marquis by all accounts makes
a fond husband & a son I understand has lately crowned your felicity, but my lady is not this bliss too per-

fect to endure, do you not dread an interruption, a profound calm is generally succeeded by a storm, do you not know of one whose appearance would utterly blast all this course of extatic pleasure?" "Miss Foxley, Miss Foxley," murmured Marian in a scarcely audible tone "don't torture me so for heaven's for my mother's sake whom you once respected end this suspense & let me know the worst Is he returned you" answered
"I will show ~~she~~ Miss Foxley ringing the bell which was almost instantly answered by the servant maid
"Tell the ~~young~~ gentleman in the next room I wish to speak with him said she. [illegible]. the girl departed & almost immediately after a young man entered the room, he was tall & genteelly formed with brown hair wild dark eyes & a handsome though meagre countenance. "Mr Henry" said Miss Foxley "allow me to introduce your early friend Marian Hume to you [now]" unfortunately she bears another surname but that is not my fault." he approached the marchioness
& said madam'
who sat with her face buried in her hands "Permit me to announce myself as that long absent Henry Percy who once at least was honoured with your regard. At the sound of his voice, she raised her head, looked at him fixedly for some minutes & then replied "This is not, cannot be Henry, he was younger, fairer, his voice softer. ~~this person~~ Miss Foxley you are deceiving me this person scarcely resembles him in the least" "That may be" answered the Governess "yet not withstanding he is Henry Percy your Henry Percy & no other" "I deny it, here is his picture (taking a portrait from her bosom) compare them & tell me where the similitude lies." "Madam" interposed the young man "I do not wonder
long
at your denial of my identity. The lapse of time & a ~sojourn in foreign climates must necessarily have produced a vast change, but though ~I may be altered externally yet within all is as it ever was which is I fear more than can be said of some others" "Do not insult me sir" said Marian the deadly white to which her cheek had faded giving place to a bright flush of anger "I shall believe the evidence of my senses rather than your assertions" "Since you will not credit my word" replied he "look at this token and reject its testimony if you dare" so saying he put into her hand a small silver box, she opened it, a
bring
single glance at its contents seemed to [illegible] sudden & forcible conviction for with a faint shriek she sank back ~~lifel~~ in the chair almost deprived of animation "Now perjured one do you acknowledge me?" asked Mr Percy with bitter emphasis "I do, I do but oh! spare me for one week give me
day
at least that time for thought, for consideration" "Not ~~an~~ [illegible], not an hour will I spare you my claim is legal & I will enforce it now. the marchioness then fell on her knees & with streaming eyes & clasped hands implored a reprieve however short, her extreme agony seemed at length to move him. "Rise madam" said he "you shall have a week's delay on condition that you promise not to consult with the marquis of Douro during that time & added Miss Foxley "on condition that you likewise promise to return here tomorrow night in order to receive important information respecting yourself my lady which you do not at present appear to be in a situation to listen to." "I will promise anything" exclaimed she grateful for this temporary relief "but of what nature is the information you allude to Miss Foxley "I merely wish to let you know who & what you are, a circumstance of which you have hitherto been ignorant. "Cannot I hear it now? No it is too late, the dawn is already rising" Marian then after some further conversation took her leave
Ned
She found ~anxiously awaiting her return in the street by the dim light of the breaking day

they hastily trod the path to Wellesley house where fortunately they arrived unobserved Ned then after receiving his young lady's cordial thanks which he valued even more than the solid reward which accompanied them, retired to enjoy in peace the refreshment of undisturbed slumber. the marchioness likewise sought her pillow but sorrow & sad thought banished sleep far from the stately couch where she lay.

CHAPTER THE III.ʳᵈ

On the night ~~of~~ after that spoken of in my last chapter the drawing room at Ellrington House exhibited a more tranquil scene than it usually does. instead of the dark political [Design], turbulent & boisterous wine party or [illegible] [bewildering] crowd of Fashion's bright devotees. Two persons alone the Lord & lady of the mansion sat one on each side of the cheerful & tranquil hearth Afew wax tapers on the mantle-piece shining amongst a hundred sparkling decorations aided by the ~~clear~~ blaze of a clear fire furnished light sufficient to enable lord Ellrington to peruse a treatise on the present state of society & ~~lady Ellrin~~ his wife to decipher the characters of a Persian Poem. At length the former after several muttered expressions of contempt for his author threw down the work & said "Come Zenobia give up poring over that absurd [passion] you are at there I dare say if one could read it its the rarest trash in nature" "Indeed Ellrington you are mistaken finer sentiments were never embodied in language, but what book have you been reading all this time?" "A translation into the English ~~language~~ ᵗᵒⁿᵍᵘᵉ of an ass's bray" "Indeed then you ~~have been~~ ʷᵉʳᵉ less profitably employed than myself, I was construing the song of a nightingale to his favourite Rose" "And pray what is the [illegible] name of the idiot who has conceived that surpassingly magnificent idea" [Ferdoona] one of the greatest Poets Persia ever produced." "And do you really Zenobia admire such groveling nonsense?" "most undoubtedly I do" "Well women are the most incomprehensible creatures on [illegible] earth, sometimes you seem to be possessed of considerable sense & discernment & then again you commit acts & utter speeches which ᵃʳᵍᵘᵉ a great weakness if not a total deprivation of intellect" "~~What Ale~~ Granting it is so Alexander might I not say the same of you? how often during the revolution of a year are you as rational as at present" "If I were not in a particularly easy humour tonight that sentence would stick in my throat Zenny" "Would it? & most likely in that case a bottle of wine would be necessary to wash it down" "Probably, but tell me now I think on it, ʷʰᵃᵗ ᵐᵃᵏᵉˢ ʸᵒᵘ ~~why do you~~ hide all your [illegible] hair under that singularly formed ᶜᵃᵖ which you have lately worn" "Fashion my lord & the caprice of custom" "What does Fashion induce the ladies to destroy their beauty?" Sometimes, but since you dislike it the defect is easily remedied" so saying she plucked out the comb which confined her hair & immediately a cloud of raven tresses fell down in rich profusion over her neck & shoulders. "There" said Ellrington after a moment's silence "You look like yourself now it is astonishing what a difference the presence or absence of a few curled locks makes" Pleased with her attention to his wishes he found himself in a better & more amicable humour than any which had soothed his stormy soul for many a long year when just as he had reached the acme of suavity a rap was heard at the door "come in" said he & the servant who stood without was startled at the gentleness of tone in which these words were pronoun-

ced, as generally when he ventured to disturb his master thus a volley of oaths & curses [illegible] the reward of his pains. Timidly opening the door he announced that a person wished to speak with Lord
Ellrington. "A Person! & pray what kind of a one is it coming here at this time of night?" "It is a woman
my lord & I believe a young one, though she keeps her face so covered with a handkerchief that I can't see
it distinctly" "Hey some mystery well show her into the library & say I'll come directly." "What can the
creature possibly want" said lady Zenobia "I think Ellrington it was foolish of you not to send a denial." Oh!
nonsense Zenny she may have something particular to tell me you know." When lord Ellrington entered the library he perceived a slender female figure attired in a silk mantle & a large straw hat
which had fallen back & discovered a luxuriant flow of beautiful chesnut ringlets, her face was turned
away & partially hidden with the palms of her small white hands "Well my girl" said he "what is your
business with me" at first she made no answer he repeated the question. she then slowly lifted her head
& discovered a countenance which bright with blushes & formed in the most exquisite mould of youthful love
liness appeared an object so fair & fascinating that the lofty nobleman could not restrain an exclamation
of surprise. After gazing at her a moment with an astonished air he said "do I deceive myself or is this
the peerless marchioness of Douro "my lord your conjecture is right" replied she at once seeming to [ill.]
throw of the bashfulness which had before oppressed her & fearlessly meeting his fixed gaze with an eye that
sparkled almost with the light of insanity" "I am that unhappy woman" "And to what am I indebted
for this [ill.] unexpected though most welcome pleasure" "To Desperation my lord nothing short of that
should have made me humble myself so" "I am sorry for that fair lady [ill.] I hoped you were come of free will
but tell me in what I can serve you it shall not be said that the prettiest woman in Verdopolis asked
my assistance in vain". "Do not talk so" my lord Ellrington exclaimed Marian while a sudden shudder ran
through her whole frame "Knowing what I know such light language sounds horrible" "And what do you
know [ill.] my lady?" "What I would not tell you for worlds & what I am come here in order to confirm
though I fear it scarce needs confirmation" "This is mysterious language I do not understand it
but you will ere long. tell me my lord have you not a casket belonging to the late lady Percy which
up to this day you have never been able to open?" "I have but how in the name of the heavens, the earth
the seas & all that are therein did you obtain knowledge of it? "That I cannot explain to you at present
my lord permit me only to see the box & I will show you a method of opening it" "Well I really cannot
refuse a request from such lips so [allow] permit me my lady marchioness to conduct you into the appartment
were the object of your curiosity is kept" with these words he offered to take her hand, she however
withdrew it with an apparently involuntary movement of repulsion" "What" said he scowling furiously
"Do you dare to reject in disdain that courtesy which it was almost a degradation condescension in me to
offer?" "I was wrong" replied Marian bursting into tears. "You may take my hand lord Ellrington for
I fear you have a right to command me in every-thing" The last words were uttered in so low a tone
as to be inaudible to his lordship, her tears however softened him as he imagined them to arise from a
fear dread of his anger he [ill.] therefore accepted the hand which otherwise might perhaps now have been
declined & taking up a candle led her out of the room. They passed in silence across the entrance Hall
ascended the Grand Staircase & trod with noiseless step the matted floor of a long gallery at the ter-

mination of which was a door, this lord ^E^ unlocked & they entered a small appartment pannelled with black

oak, in the centre of it stood a table covered with papers & in one corner an ~~cabin~~ elaborately carved cabin

et, in which lay [~~illegible~~] ^four^ swords, three sheathed and one naked & above them hung a large banner blood-red

& bearing for its device a ^skull & cross-bones^ ~~death's head~~ in black. "This" said the nobleman after having again locked the

door "is my sanctum sanctorum Lady marchioness" he paused & looked steadily upon her as if to see what

impression the scene produced. It was indeed a strangely awful situation for poor Marian to be placed

in, there she stood at the dead hour of the night alone & face to face with that dark, stern man whose

mighty talents & still mightier crimes will hereafter appall the muse of History as she records them

A deeping & boding silence reigned around interrupted only by the faint dull sound of a closing door [or]

hurried tread from some distant part of the vast mansion, sounds that only served to intimate

that help if needed was too far off to be obtained. Cold ran the blood to that youthful lady's heart as she

thought on these things, but terror so restrained her tongue & fettered her limbs while under the in-

fluence of that searching falcon eye that she neither breathed a word or moved a finger. "How do you

like it he continued" with a sardonic smile ^lifting the lamp^ drawing up his ~~tall~~ ^lofty^ form to all its majestic height

"You see those four swords? & that red flag on the cabinet yonder," She bowed "Well now my lady I'll

tell you what they mean "this is the blade I wielded in my youth when I killed Negroes for Wellington

this is the weapon that helped me in exile it is drunk with the blood of merchants' by sea & land, ^&^ th[is]

not many years since made Alexander the first tremble on his mountain throne those three

are all sheathed they have done their work they have slain their thousands & tens of thousands &

now they may rest. but for this other look at it my lady, look at it well, see how sharp & bright & glit-

tering ^it is^ not a spot of blood not a streak of rust blackens it. this is a virgin sword, it has pierced no heart

freed ^no spirit^ but it lies bare & ready, it bides its time, a voice & a power is in that weapon. the voice shall

speak the doom of nations the ~~doom~~ ^power^ shall execute it. And by the strength of what arm shall it do these

things he continued suddenly laying his hand on her shoulder with a force that made her tremble " &

for what prize [~~illegible~~] will the great game be played. mine is the arm a crown is the prize." he

paused a moment & then went on again in a lower tone "As for that flag it is the pennon of the

black Rover, for seven years it swept the seas the dreaded the invincible. In storm & sunshine, war & mirth

the battle & the Festival, she remained unhurt, unchanged, When the waves were strewed with the tem-

pest torn fragments of the merchantman & the man of war, my good ship. their dread & scourge, spread

her white sail & like a haunting spirit of the deep proudly breasted those waters that none else dared

look upon. men said she was charmed against wind & wave & they spoke truth for I trod her deck & direc

ted her course therefore Destiny with her triple shield ever hovered round—" "but stop am I a madman

or an idiot to talk thus to you humph I fear I have been letting out. but it is easy to prevent consequences

Kneel down my ~~la~~ marchioness of Douro, kneel this instant, dare you resist, there that is right, you must

excuse the push I gave you but it is always best to obey me at once without hesitation. "Now swear by

the head of that old man whom you worship never to whisper in mortal ear one word of what I have been

saying this night, Swear or —" "I do swear" said she in a faint voice "That is well get up, you are an obedient

& praiseworthy girl & if I had the management of you would soon arrive at the perfection of feminine meek ness & humility. Marian rose & stood before the imperious Nobleman she was deadly pale & might have passed for a beautiful marble statue, had not the tremor which shook every limb indicated that her form was of living flesh & blood. Lord Ellrington again fixed his eye [~~illegible~~] ^{on her} & seemed to take pleasure in witnessing the profound awe which his keen gaze inspired. At last after torturing her thus for some minutes, he broke out into a long & loud burst of laughter. She stept back & looked at him doubtingly as if she thought his brain disturbed, "Well" he exclaimed as soon as the exhaustion arising from his strange fit of merriment would permit him to speak "Have I frightened you my lady? Come nonsense cheer up. One would think you were never spoken to harshly or looked at sternly before. Pray does the marquis never discipline you a little in this way? Confess the truth now is he not sometimes rather crusty & overbearing?" My lord ~~exclaim~~^{stat}ed Marian while an indignant blush crimsoned her snowy brow & faded cheek "I will not hear my husband's name mentioned thus even by you satanically proud as you are—" She would have said more but the half-formed words died away on her lips & with them the transient flash of spirit likewise vanished "Satanically proud" muttered lord Ellrington ~~Where you ar~~ after her that is daring you forget I think my lady where you ~~were~~^{are} & how situated, but methinks you need not pretend to be so thin-skinned as it regards the marquis at the moment when you are committing what in his eyes would unquestionably appear a_^^{most} deadly offence, for I do not think he is acquainted with this midnight visit to Ellrington House" Marian made no reply to this cutting remark she only sighed deeply. A Pause now ensued during which lord E. slowly paced the room, it was sometime before she ventured ~~again~~ to interrupt him by again referring to the business which had occasioned her visit. at length summoning resolution she said hesitatingly "can your lordship permit me to look at the casket now?" without answering, he strode directly ~~from~~^{to} the cabinent & taking a key from his pocket unlocked it. a multitude of miscellaneous articles were contained in the different divisions but in one more carefully arranged than the rest there appeared ~~a box of~~ ^{an} ivory ^{box} inlaid with silver, a long braided lock of beautiful light brown hair, a lady's ~~gold~~ watch, & a miniature portrait of a beautiful woman set in a massive gold frame, richly decorated with jewels. he took the box & ~~placed~~^{put} it in^{to} her hand. she moved a few places from him towards the table on which the lamp was placed & having opened the casket by means of a secret spring took from it a paper that formed the whole of its contents. this she glanced hastily over & then suddenly & before lord E could prevent her ~~tore it into a hundred fragments~~ consumed it in the flame of the lamp exclaiming when she had done "Thank God that evidence is destroyed" How dare you said he approaching her with angry strides & laying his hand as if by instinct on a pistol which appeared half hidden in his breast "If you were a man I'd blow you to atoms for that action this moment" "Do it now" said Marian perfectly undaunted by his manner "And rid me of a life which I have lost the power of enjoying" "No" he replied thrusting back the pistol "I'll not kill you, but I'll do what perhaps in your present state of mind would be almost as bad, I'll keep you locked up here till you_^^{tell me} & that truly the contents of the paper which you have just destroyed" "That I will never do, every fresh view ~~of you~~ which I obtain of your conduct determines me more against_^^{it}" "Is the silly girl mad" said lord Ellrington with a gloomy frown "Has she forgotten who & what I am" "No my lord I have not but the sen-

118

timents which I cannot help entertaining against you, will force their way despite of all my efforts to restrain them" "[Note] then you may take the consequences of your want of [illegible] self-government & continue here with me at least till the morning-light. if you behave well during the next five or six hours I may perhaps permit you to return home in [time] to explain your absence to the marquis as you best can" In vain did Marian endeavour by entreaties remonstrances & even tears, to turn him from his purpose he was inexorable and during the remainder of that night she was compelled to continue an unwilling prisoner listening to the keen taunts, false insinuations & detested gallantry of her stern jailor. At last just as the lamp was beginning to wane before the first pale beams of dawn which shone faintly through the single lofty & narrow window with which the appartment was lighted, a hesitating knock was heard at the door. "Who's there" thundered lord Ellrington "It is only I" replied the voice of lady Zenobia his wife in very subdued tones "I wished to know ₐAlexander whether you intended to retire to rest at all before morning or not" "And how dare you wish to know anything about the matter, off to your bed this instant without reply" Zenobia understood the accent in which her husband spoke & withdrew immediately "Now" said he turning to the marchioness "I will per allow your little ladyship to depart, come along". Gladly she followed him as after unlocking the door he led the way through gallery, hall & passage to the Grand Entrance, this he unfastened with his own hands. Marian did not wait for any farewell ceremonies but darting past him cleared the steps at a spring, fled down the street with the speed & lightness of a roe and was out of sight in a twinkling. [ill.] an effusion of golden light filled the east before she reached Wellesley House, all however ʷᵃˢ still silent around that lordly mansion & when she rung the bell at the private door it was opened by Mina. "Oh my lady" exclaimed that faithful handmaiden "I am so glad you are come I have passed such a night of suspense & misery on your account as no one ever did before scarcely" "Did the marquis return home last night?" asked her mistress "Yes he did at four o'clock, I then thought that [ill.] your absence could not miss being discovered & gave up all for lost, but most fortunately he went to his own bed-room & therefore everything is still safe you know my lady "Thank Heaven & the great Genii who watched over me" ejaculated the marchioness. "Now Mina go to bed as I am sure you must be tired, I can undress myself." Mina then left the room & in a few minutes her young mistress oppressed with grief & watching was enjoying a temporary oblivion of her sorrows in the repose of sleep.

CHAPTER THE IV.ᵗʰ

She had scarcely rested three hours when Mina again stood by her bed-side "My lady" said she "will you rise now, the marquis has sent up to say that breakfast is waiting. "What o'clock is it" asked Marian "Nine" my lady "O then I will rise of course, how provoking that he should have to wait for me" Marian the marchioness was soon dressed as her attire in the morning is dictated by the very spirit of tasteful simplicity & a few touches brought her soft, naturally curling glossy tresses into becoming order. When the business of the toilette was over she proceeded to attend the marquis, her heart beat fast [illegible] as she approached the breakfast room for she had not seen him since the interview mentioned in one of my former chapters when he left her in anger sternly prohibiting any intercourse with Miss Foxley & how had this prohibition been attended to?

Arthur as she entered the appartment was seated with his back to the door engaged in the perusal of a newspaper. her tread was too light to attract attention & she feared to address him unspoken to uncertain whether he had yet forgotton his wrathful mood, so she quietly took her seat at the ~~breakfast~~ table & began to arrange the material for breakfast. The tinkle of Porcelain & silver soon roused him, he looked up with a smile & said "Well Marian wont you bid me good morning, I hope you are not in a bad temper at being [ill.] ^{called} out of your bed so early" "No indeed Arthur on the contrary I am ashamed of myself for having made you wait so long. Forgive me however as I am not often so deficient in punctuality" I'll consider about" replied he playfully "Perhaps your request may be granted for I do not find myself inclined to be very angry on that score" my brother's breakfast is generally protracted to the space of about an hour and a half as [illegible] of eating straight forward like other people, he sits maundering over the morning papers and as my landlord ~~would~~ says taking a sup & a bite at intervals of about a quarter of an hour each. Some ladies of my acquaintance would raise a fine hubbub if they had to wait for their husbands such an unconscionable length of time, but the marchioness of Douro who considers herself honoured in being permitted to attend the beck of her lord & master [illegible] when she has finished her own slight repast [ill.] usually takes up some piece of ornamental ~~needle~~-^{fancy}work & continues patiently plying the needle with her small slight fingers until the last leading article of the last newspaper is concluded. this morning her labour was interrupted by [illegible] frequent & deep sighs every time one of these indications of grief escaped her lips. The marquis though unseen by his wife just lifted his eyes from the paper & surveyed her with a most peculiar expression & when they fell again on the speech or paragraph he seemed for ^a~~the~~ moment rather engaged with his own thoughts than the sense of what he was reading. At length like all sublunary things Arthur's breakfast had an end. the ^{service}[ill.] being cleared away & all set to rights by an attendant footman, Marian was about to leave the room in order to visit ^{her}~~the~~ nursery, when suddenly the marquis rose and coming close up to her took her hand "Marian" said he after a momentary ^{silence}~~pause~~ "you look very pale this morning What is the reason of it" "I – I – did not sleep very well last night" stammered ^{she}while her frame trembled like an aspen leaf. "That is not all, it could not occasion this tremor & what makes your hand turn so cold within mine "I am sure, I do not know" replied Marian endeavouring to force a smile, but the attempt only brought a tear into her dark blue eye. The marquis looked at her as if he would have pierced to the farthest recesses of her heart & said in a low [ill.] thrilling voice "Have you disobeyed my mandates, have you seen that woman & are her chains again rivetted round you?" There was a pause, Marian seemed almost annihilated, the rapidly varying hue of her countenance proclaimed the violence of those emotions with which her soul was now rent. she could not answer she could not even look up at her imperious lord, but stood voiceless and motionless like one petrified. "It is well" said he dropping her hand & sternly folding his arms "I understand that silence, you have chosen to follow the direction of your own weak inclinations & to disregard my wishes I have told you before that the consequences of such a line of conduct would be an immediate separation, it is my custom to make my words & deeds conformable therefore this very day & before three hours elapse the travelling carriage will be in readiness to take you to my father's country-house in Wellington's land. Good bye, this is in all probability our last interview for I cannot love a disobedient wife" "Arthur, my dearest Arthur

don't leave me thus, you would not think so hardly of me if you knew all" "Tell me all then" said he hastily
& taking his hand from the door lock which he was just about to turn "I dare not" "And why" "because I am
bound by a promise not to consult you for a week & at the end of that time all consultation will I fear be
in vain for then I must leave you for ever." The marquis was ~~about~~ going to answer when the door open
ed & his Grace the Duke of Wellington entered. he halted as Bobadil would say on the threshold & after looking keenly from Arthur to Marian & noting the attitude & countenance of each, said in a quiet tone
of inquiry "what ails you both, have I arrived just in time to witness a slight specimen of matrimonial felicity Eh? There was no answer, the marquis only moved away to a window & began to watch the
clouds as they sailed slowly by. his Grace then adressed himself more particularly to the lady "What
have you done Marian" said he "to bring that lowering and tempestuous cloud over your husband's countenance" Marian burst into tears "I did not mean to offend him" sobbed she "but—" but what love I
trust this is not unnecessary severity on his part" "No, No, No, he only wishes to know something which I
cannot tell him" "And what is that something? can you tell me? "Yes said the marchioness looking up
while a smile began to illumine her still glistening eyes "I think I will your Grace will know how to advise
me better than anyone else & I have not promised to keep it a secret from you" "Come then child sit
down [illegible] by me & let us hear this ~~great~~ wonderful secret. Marian sat down beside the duke as he desired her
for a little while she was silent & seemed to be collecting her faculties & summoning resolution for
some great effort, the composure of resignation rather than peace at length overspread her features
but there was still a wildness in her look & a tremble in her voice as she said "my lord Duke, I am
not your son's wife, I am not Sir Alexander Hume's daughter." At these words the marquis of Douro started as if he had received a shock of electricity. he turned round & would have spoken but his father restrained
him saying "hush Arthur, not a word from your lips or I shall desire you to quit the room instantly, Now
my love he continued ~~explain to me in the~~ addressing Marian "explain to me in the first place how you
are not my son's wife. About five years ago" replied she "A short time before my [ill.] mother or her whom
until lately I considered as such died & when she was fast wasting under that languishing disease which
at length destroyed her, I was one day summoned to her chamber. She was sitting up supported by
pillows & near the bed-side stood Mr Hall our private chaplain, Miss Foxley my governess, whom your
Grace may perhaps remember to have seen (the Duke nodded assent) "and Henry Percy, the youngest
son of lord Ellrington whose country seat was situated not far from Badey-Hall. he was a boy of about
my own age & had been my playfellow as long as I could remember. "Marian" said my mother when
I came to her "you have often heard me speak of the late lady Percy have you not" I said I had & she
went on "She was my dearest friend all her wishes are now sacred to me & there is one of them which
this day I desire to see fulfilled. On her death bed shortly after you & Henry were born she expressed a
wish that in rembrance of our friendship you would be united in case of your both arriving at years of
discretion. I am now dying & tomorrow Henry will depart on a voyage to a distant part of the world
whence he may never return. I should like therefore to see you betrothed now in my presence & if my
always hitherto dutiful daughter would render her mother's last moments happy she will consent to bestow her hand on one who I doubt not will hereafter render her a happy wife." I could not refuse to

comply with my dear mother's request when I knew how soon the grave & coffin were to hide her forever from my sight & besides even had the powerful motive of obedience to her been absent I could have
found no excuse in my own inclinations to sanction a refusal ~~for~~ though I did not then know what love
was yet I had always liked Henry Percy who was a handsome & affectionate boy for his good nature & kind
disposition. We accordingly pledged our faith before the chaplain & each gave the other a token by which when
we met again at some future period we might recognize each other. The next day he set out on his
long journey & a few weeks after my mother was carried to the tomb. Time past on & I heard nothing
of Henry till the third year after his departure when one morning Miss Foxley was looking over a newspaper in which she showed me a paragraph announcing the wreck of the Mermaid the ship which
Henry had sailed on among some distant & unknown countries called the South-Sea Islands & the destruction of all her crew including Lieutenant Percy son of the celebrated Alexander Rogue. I mourned for Henry's death but neither long nor bitterly. Absence had caused his image & the calm child-like
affection ^with^ which I viewed him to grow dim in my mind & memory. Twelve months after I saw the
marquis, new feelings, passions which I had never till then experienced arose in my heart. I need
not tell your Grace that all things were settled for my union with your son when in what must
have appeared to you an unaccountably capricious manner I suddenly stopped the preparations & declared that I never could consent to be his wife. I had however a reason & one sufficiently conclusive
Three days before my marriage was to have taken. & while Miss Foxley was engaged in making my bridal dress she received a letter from a shipmate of Henry's with whom she was acquainted declaring that the
story of the Mermaid's wreck was all false & that both vessel & crew were well & pursuing a prosperous voyage. You cannot my lord I think blame me if after this though with the greatest violence to my own
feelings I broke off all intercourse with your son. None can tell what I suffered when I saw him day by day
pining for my sake but Duty strongly pointed out to me the path which I ought to pursue & I dared not
turn aside. Your opinion of my caprice must have been confirmed when after several months of steady
rejection I at once and suddenly yielded to his entreaties. there was a cause also for this but I scarcely dare
tell it you lest you should suspect me of an inclination [~~ill.~~] ^for^ romance" The Duke encouraged her to continue & she went on. "Late one calm summer's evening I wandered out to a distant part of the grounds
& sitting down in a little wild alcove which was my favourite retreat began sorrowfully to brood over the image of Arthur & the sad certainty that I should never be his. I thought & wept till it began to grow dark
& then fearful of passing through the park at night & disturbing the deer & wild cattle from their slumbers I rose to return & had advanced a little way up the forest walk where the ~~arbor~~ alcove was erected
when a voice faint & mournful whispered my name. I turned & saw standing under the arch I had
just left the dim figure of a man. "Who is there" I asked in some alarm "instead of answering he glided towards me. I shrieked out he beckoned me to be silent & said in very hollow tones which I shudder even
now to recollect "Look at me Marian & know your Henry. Just then the moon broke from a cloud & her
light falling through the branches revealed to me a form & face which bore ^indeed^ a slight resemblance to Henry
but it was so changed & distored that I should never have recognized it of my own accord. The hair & clothes

were all wet & dripping, the eyes wide open but void of all expression save one of ghastliness the face blue &
livid & all the features swollen. I was too much appalled at this horrid change to answer. So I lie Marian
among the Coral Islands of the South-Sea. Listen not to Deceivers, fear not that I shall return [ill.], Death &
the waters of a vast deep, chain me to my place, be happy & think of your first love no more. The wraith
then walked into air before me & filled with horror I hastened back to the house. On arriving there I related
what I had seen to Miss Foxley she strongly endeavoured to persuade me that it was all the fruit of my own
excited imagination, but finding my belief in the reality of the apparition fixed & likewise my determination
to act according to its counsel, she grew angry & said left me saying she was hoped that if I did marry the
marquis my repentance hereafter would be deep & bitter. three weeks subsequent to this I was married
Arthur shortly after our union dismissed Miss Foxley which I was very glad of as her sullen looks & threatening [scowls] filled me with an undefined feeling of fear. Since that time I have received no intelligence
from her till about two days ago when the marquis informed me that he had seen her in the City and
warned me against holding any communication with her. The same day a letter was brought me
from her saying that if I did not wish the whole of a certain transaction to come out I would condescend
marchioness as I was to visit my old Governess at her lodgings in Harley-Street. I went for I dared
not do otherwise & there I saw that Henry Percy whom till then I had supposed buried in the sea. He was
so changed & looked so dark & wild & meagre that at first I denied his identity but I was soon but too well
convinced by the production of that very token which five years since I had given him as a pledge of my
eternal faith. he would claimed his right over me that instant, by tears & entreaties I however gained
a reprieve of a week. On condition that during that time I would not consult with my husband on the
subject & that I would return to Harley Street next day in order to learn an important secret concerning myself. At the second interview she Miss Foxley informed me that I was not the daughter of
Sir Alexander Hume." "Who then?" I asked "The late ladies Hume & Percy" she replied "were as you know
most intimate friends. As a sign of their love for & confidence in each other they agreed when you &
Henry were born to exchange children & each bring up the other's child as their own. the affair was
managed so dexterously that none but my self knew anything of it & till this moment you have looked up to Dr Hume as your father, when in reality no less a person than Lord Ellrington stands in that
relation to you. This information affected me so deeply that I fainted. On recovering I told Miss Foxley that
unless she could bring proof of her assertion I should consider all I had just heard in the light of a
malignant falsehood. She then informed me that there was a written agreement of the affair
inclosed in a casket of lady Percy's which was fastened by a secret spring [concealed] in a particular part
which she described to me & that most probably from the difficulty of discovering this spring lord
Ellrington yet retained the box unopened" Half maddened by the idea of being that man's child whom of
all others I most dreaded & detested I [ill.] scarcely knowing what I did to Ellrington-House & there by
entreaties I prevailed on his lordship to show me the casket. I opened it, found the fatal, document glanced over its
& in a moment of anguish consumed it in the flame of a candle which stood on the table, now my
lord" she continued "you know all my secret & may if you can fathom the depth & weigh the burden of

123

that misery under which my reason at times seems to totter. I hate explanation & therefore shall condense what I have further to say into as brief a space as possible. When Marian had finished the marquis asked her to describe to him the token by which she had recognized Henry Percy "It was" replied she "a small gold ring with a crystal stone containing a little of my hair braided & my name written on the inside." "The vile old witch" exclaimed Arthur she bought it in Lapis's shop & that fellow whom you saw is no more the person you took him to be than I am. as for the talk about Lord Ellrington I doubt not it is a scandalous lie & so I'll make her confess before the day is at an end." He then rang the bell & ordered three or four of the servants to go immediately to Harley Street & take Miss Foxley & whoever they might find with her into custody, they soon returned accompanied by the Governess & her male accomplice whom my father & brother instantly recognized as Edward Percy the well known scamp & oldest brother to the youth whose character he had assumed. he unblushingly ~~confess~~ declared that his only motive for joining in the fraud was to extort a sum of money & Miss Foxley finding herself thus deserted by her assistant, confessed the falsity of all she had pretended & explained the mystery of the paper in the casket by saying that such an agreement had really existed between the Ladies Hume & Percy but had never been put in practice on account of their husband's refusing to consent. my father then told her that if she wished to escape punishment for her wickedness she must instantly leave Africa for some distant country & never set foot on its shores again. "I give you your choice" said the Duke "between two evils [illegible] Exile or the pillory choose that which you consider the least." She chose the former & was accordingly shipped off the next day. as for Edward Percy my father gave him ten sovereigns for his candid confession & dismissed him well satisfied Do you forgive my involuntary disobedience now Arthur?" asked the once more [illegible] happy Marian when all was settled. A smile & a kiss answered her more satisfactorily than words & thus ends my Tale of the Secret

LILY HART

It was on the Evening of the memorable sixteenth of March, the day of the great ~~rebellion~~ insurrection, that Mrs Hart a respectable widow lady & her daughter Lily sat by the [ill.] parlour fire-side of their quiet & modest mansion situated in one of the remote suburbs of Verdopolis. They had passed the day in a state of the most intense & feverish anxiety hourly expecting that the flames of war which were raging with such violence in other parts of the city would spread to the obscure quater in which they dwelt. Happily however about three o'clock p.m. the incessant thunder of distant artillery which till then they had heard pealing from the far off Eastern division began to dye away. the cloud of smoke which hung so gloomily between earth & heaven waxed less dense, the tumultuous roar of battle grew fainter & intelligence soon arrived that the rebellion had at length been completely put down by Government. hours elapsed before the two terrified Females could free themselves from the flutter of excitement in which they had been kept all day. but when night fell down and all continued quiet, when several fresh messengers confirmed the good news & when many of those who had been engaged in the combat returning to their homes declared that the army of rebels was utterly cut off, they began to feel themselves reassured & after bolting the doors & fastening the windows of the house ventured for the first time since morning to partake of a slight meal which Bessie their only servant had managed though half-dead with fear to prepare. When it was concluded both drew near to the fire. As yet they felt too unsettled to engage in their usual occupations of reading or sewing, but sat ~~for~~ talking over the fearful events of the day & conjecturing the probable consequences of this unsuccessful attempt against good Government. While they were thus employed Lily sudden ly stopped short in the midst of a sentence she was uttering. "Listen mama" said she. "Do you not hear a noise in the garden." Her mother listened "I do" she replied "it sounds like the moan of some one in pain, perhaps it may proceed from some poor wounded creature & if so it is our duty to assist him" with these words she stepped to a little glass door which opened into the garden, Lily followed her mother, it was a clear & still night, the moon & stars were shining most brilliantly in a perfectly unclouded Heaven & their descending beams revealed the form of a human being stretched on the grass near a little wicket which was open. Mrs Hart called to the prostrate figure but received no answer she then went up to him & took his hand it was very cold, he had ceased moaning & now lay motionless. "I fear he is dead" said the benevolent lady in a tone of compassion "but hasten Lily & tell Bessie to run instantly for the nearest surgeon. "I know something of the art of surgery" said a voice close at hand while a tall figure entered by the open wicket "And if my skill would be of any use it is at your service madam Who are you sir?" asked she in some alarm at this sudden intrusion "An officer in the Grand Army of Verdopolis madam & one whom no individual of the fair sex needs to fear" Encouraged by the soft & gentle accent in which the stranger spoke, she expressed her gratitude for his timely offer of assistance & soon the wounded man was with the additional aid of Bessie conveyed into the snug little parlour & safely deposited on a sofa. As the candle-light fell on his pallid features the officer uttered an exclamation of surprise "I know this person said he, he is my dearest friend. I trust to God he yet lives if not Africa has this day sustained a great loss" He then hastened to revive him by means of stimulants & cordial waters which Mrs Hart liberally supplied. Gradually he returned to life & on opening his eyes stared wildly round & would have spoken but his millitary medical attendant strictly forbade him to utter a word. On examination his wound was found to consist in a bayonet stab in the right side, it was not deep & most fortunately the vital parts remained uninjured. "By what name shall I call your friend sir asked Mrs Hart when the wound was staunched. & bandaged & the poor sufferer put to bed. "Mr Seymour" replied the officer after a moment's consideration. And my name is Colonel Percival, if I could venture to urge so bold a request madam I should wish him to remain here till he is completely cured I will be your guarantee for the reimbursement of such expenses as you may incur on his account Mrs Hart assured him of her perfect willingness to permit the stranger's sojourn & then after promising to call again next morning Colonel Percival took his leave "What a handsome man that officer is" said ~~Colonel P~~ Lily Hart when he was gone, "I never saw such dark & sparkling eyes or such a magnificent form & face but he looks very young to be a Colonel "He does my dear" replied her mother "most probably however he is a scion of some noble family ~~and they you know obtain preferment readily~~ At least I should conjecture so from his lofty & patrician appearance & they you know obtain preferment early. Days & weeks passed away & Mr Seymour recovered rapidly under the ~~care~~ ^treatment^ of his friend who ~~treated~~ [ill.] attended him with the most assiduous & constant [illegible] care. The invalid's manners at first were not very prepossessing in the opinion of his kind Hostesses, he appeared cold & distant ~~seemed~~ & seemed to take all the attention bestowed upon him as his right. but upon longer acquaintance this chilly reserve thawed almost entirely away. As his wound healed he became more agreeable & when at length he was able to leave his bed-room & sit in the arm-chair by the little parlour-hearth. Lily wondered how she could ever have thought him either a plain or a proud man. In person he was very tall & so erect as to appear at times rather stiff & formal his features were regularly formed, his forehead lofty & open. his eyes of a dark grey coulour. deep-set & piercing. a general air of dignified gravity prevaded his whole countenance & not withstanding his youth for he did not appear to be above twenty-five or six years of age became him extremely well. He never laughed but the contrast of his usual sobriety imparted an uncommon graciousness to his smile. but not withstanding all this his disposition was evidently turned to a fondness for domestic life & female society. he would sit in a rustic seat in the garden ^when he was able^ weaving a garland of roses for the head of Lily or the neck of her favourite lap-dog. He constructed a pretty moss house & adorned it with shells & pebbles. at times though not often he would accompany Miss Hart's [ill.] Guitar with his power^ful^ yet melodious voice & regularly every morning he gave her lessons in the Italian language in which he appeared to be a proficient & which she was studying. Then in the evenings when the curtains were let down & the fire burned bright, while the ladies sat at their needle-work Mr Seymour would read to them from some standard author, commenting on remarkable passages as he went on & illustrating such as were obscure, in language so lucid, so unassuming & at times so eloquent as to give them a most exalted idea of his understanding. When he became earnest in conversation which he often did [ill.] if the subject interested him, his countenance grew very animated, his eyes sparkled & his words flowed forth with freedom energy & even brilliancy. Often when he was thus awakened, Lily would drop her work gaze on him earnestly & then when the tide of inspired feeling gradually ebbed & he ~~ret~~ returned to his customary calm & stately demeanour, ^she would^ reassume it with an involuntary sigh. Mrs Hart marked this & many other little indications of her daughter's [growing] regard for their guest. When Mr Seymour spoke Lily was all rapt & earnest attention, ^when^ he was unusually grave a sympathizing sadness appeared on her face. If the slightest complaint of returning pain or weakness escaped him, she trembled lest he should relapse. & if a lighter tread or a gayer strain of conversation proclaimed improving health & spirits her joy knew no bounds. all these tokens of incipient affection were noticed by the careful mother & occasioned her many an hour of anxious ^meditation^ ~~affection~~ for though she could easily discern the state of her daughter's ~~feelings~~ mind yet that of [illegible] the stranger defied her penetration he was so sedate so guarded possessed such complete comand over himself that it was utterly impossible to read his thoughts in his countenance. True Lily was handsome enough to attract the attention of any man & so my readers would have thought had they seen her. She was about eighteen years old, rather above than under the middle size, elegantly formed with gracefully rounded limbs

& small fairy-like face & hands. her complexion was of a rich & sunny tone of coulouring. Dark, bright eyes, softened by long silken lashes, diffused a most fascinating expression over her sweet face & [ill.] harmonized well with the wild black curling^s which waved in such luxuriant clusters over her glowing vermillion cheeks. to these attractions were added a charming simplicity of dress & manner, all the re- fined accomplishments of a polite education & the more solid advantages of a useful one. Yet this lovely creature failed to excite [illegible]^{any} emotion in the in this respect almost stoical Mr Seymour beyond what was indicated by an occasional fixed gaze which was instantly withdrawn & compensated for by an addi- tional degree of Gravity & restraint. In the space of two months he was by dint of good nursing restore[d] to perfect health but yet he did not seem willing to depart. One morning while they were sitting at breakfast Colonel Percival happened to call. after a little desultory conversation he began to urge on his friend the necessity of returning to his family who he said were beginning to be very anxious about him Mr Seymour made no answer to his arguments but appeared very loath to acknowledge their justice at length the colonel said laughingly "Well if you still refuse to quit your quarters I shall begin to think some one has cast a spell round you. Perhaps my fair Lily here could furnish me with the name of the enchantress if she would." A deep blush crimsoned the young Philosopher's brow he started up directly & ex- claimed "I will go this instant, I will quit this peaceful retreat without delay. Mrs Hart allow me to offer you a very slight compensation for your unwearied kindness & attention towards me." So saying he tendered her a bank note of two hundred pounds. This however his disinterested Hostess most promptly refused in vain he implored her to accept it she would not & in the end he was compelled to return it to his pocket book Then turning to Lily he took her hand pressed it gently slipped off a valuable diamond ring which decorated his little finger placed it on hers & with a faint mournful farewell abruptly left the house. Colonel Percival looked after him a moment with a significant smile bowed gracefully to both the ladies. wished them a good morning and departed. A year elapsed & during that little space of Time Poor Lily saw many and mighty changes. She had wept the loss of a loved & loving mother whom a severe illness had in seven days time carried to her grave, she had been left destitute by the failure of a banker in whose hands the whole of her small though competent fortune was lodged & she had been forced to leave the house where she was born & brought up & now resided in a humble dwelling containing only two appartments here she endeavoured to support herself by manufacturing & selling little ornamental articles such as screens, racks.^[&c] All day long she sat engaged in the production of the most beautiful & elegant forms yet her utmost diligence could only procure her the means of a very scanty subsistence. In the mean- time [several words illegible] with grief for her dear parent's death & another deep-seated & hopeless sor row greatly impaired her health. She grew thin & pale her eye lost step lost its elasticity her eye its lustre, her cheek its bloom & in short she faded to the mere shadow of her former self. One Evening after toiling ten weary hours over scraps of card-board & shreds of gilt paper, sick at heart with her thank- less labour she rose & wrapping herself in a large mantle left her house to seek relaxation in a short walk Grateful was the freshness of the soft balmy summers Evening wind as it kissed her wasted cheek & played among her black unbraided ringlets. The golden glory of a fast westering sun lay on the distant harbour brightened its busy shores & lit up with a warm glow the rock-like structure which soars from the centre of magnificent Verdopolis. Unconscious whither her way tended she paced slowly on, gazing now at the [illegible] dazzling west now at the far of hills which shone dimly visible in the excess of radiance which suffused them & now at the dark blue waters of the seemingly waveless sea. Such an assemblage of lovely objects soon quickly calmed her griefs & excited in her mind a train of soothing meditations. Ere long she was roused from her delicious reverie by a hum of human voices & a tread of passing footsteps which warned her that she had left her own quiet quarter of the city & was entering upon a busier [ill.]. She looked up & saw that she was in the wide & splendid street called Ebor terrace, Heaven-aspiring Palaces of the most superb & imposing architecture rose on each side & seemed in their princely pride to frown away any poor plebeian who might chance to fix his eye on them. This street as my readers well know is the Grand Corso of Verdopolis & now at the fashionable hour of sunset it was crowded with hundreds of equestrians & pedestrians. Here groups of patrician Beauties, lustrous in the fascination of bright eyes, lovely lips beaming gems & nodding plumes, glided stately by & as they went a soft perfume & a sweet murmur of silver tones lingered on the breeze behind them. There a stately chariot with six or eight fiery horses passed full speed like a rushing [illegible] whirlwind & every where the noble & the beautiful moved like beings of another sphere seeming to disdain the ground on which they trod. As poor Lily looked round on the glittering forms of life & splendour, not one of whom would condescend to cast a look or waste a [ill.] thought on her she felt a sensation of utter loneliness & breathing a deep sigh turned to depart. While she was hastily retracing her steps she chanced to glance upwards at one of the majestic edifices [ill.] frowning above her & saw seated at an open window & gazing pensively at the brilliant crowds beneath the well remembered form of Mr Seymour. At this unexpected sight a smothered exclamation of joyful surprise burst from Lily's lips & a radiant light sparkled in her dark eye she stood transfixed for a moment & while yet lost in wonder & delight, he raised his eyes & they fell on her. blushing deeply she hung down her head & covered her face with her hands, when she looked again the window was closed & the welcome vision departed "Cruel man" thought she while a shower of unbidden tears gushed forth "he might have spoken one lit word to me were it only for the sake of my mother's kindness" The recollection of her mother determined Lily to visit the grave where her beloved ashes reposed & with the tardy tread of sorrow she took the way to St Michaels Cemetry. Twilight had quenched the glory of the setting sun in soft & silent shades ere she reached that huge wilderness of tombs & a pale crescent moon was gilding the gloomy groves of gigantic cypress trees as she sat down near an upright headstone of grey marble which stood close under the lofty southern wall. utterly unbroken was the frozen hush which hung over that [city] of the dead no step no voice waked an echo among the silent tombs. but soon the cathedral clock tolled the hour of vespers & then there came floating on the night ^air the swell of a solemn organ from the holy minster which stood bathed in heavy moonbeams not far distant & the sublime sound of a sacred song, as the chant died away Lily took up the tune & sang mournfully the following stanzas.

Dark is the mansion of the dead
           Dark desolate and still
Around it dwells a solemn dread
           Within a charnel chill

O mother! does thy spirit rest
           In fairer worlds than ours?
'mid tranquil valleys ever-blest
           And ever-blooming bowers?

I trust it doth for thy pale clay
           Hath found no fair abode
Shut from the happy light of day
           Pressed by the cold earth's load

Yet mother! I would rest with thee
           In thy long dreamless sleep
Though dread its mute solemnity
           All voiceless, still & deep

And I would rest my weary head
           Upon thy lifeless breast
Nor feel one shuddering thrill of dread
           At what my temples prest

Earth is a dreary void to me
           Heaven is a cloud of gloom
Then mother! let me sleep with thee
           Safe in thy stilly tomb

She ceased & throwing herself on the grassy grave wept and sobbed aloud, when this paroxysm of grief subsided she rose & was preparing to leave the cemetry when a tall & dark figure glided
from an adjoining cemetry cypress grove & stood before her. Overcome with terror at this sudden apparition she shrieked aloud. "Does Miss Hart fear him whose life she saved" said a deep calm voice
Lily answered not, but seized with sudden faintness sank on a stone which stood near. the stranger
seated himself beside her & took her passive hand. "Has my Lily forgotten the ungrateful Seymour?" he
asked in soothing accents. No never, never," was her enthusiastic reply "nor will till death separates
me from all earthly associations." "From what I have just heard." From what I have said he "you
have lost your earthly protector & are now left desolate in the world" "I am" replied she briefly. he

129

paused a moment & then said "Lily you have doubtless by this time concluded that I have lost all recollection of you & your [household], but it is not so I have striven indeed to forget you laboured night & day to erase the impress of your too dear image from my mind to this end I have sought the drawing-room & the ball-room in order to find some form of superior loveliness some mind of higher excellence than those which haunted me like a heavenly vision, but in vain not one could I discover amongst all the fairest & noblest of the land to vie with my peerless my lovely Lily. At length unable any longer to live without you I determined despite of foolish predjudice & family pride to seek out the poor widow's daughter & gain her consent to a private union. With this resolution I went about six months since to your house in the Eastern suburbs but it was empty & none knew whither you were gone. Since that time I have sought you but in vain till this evening when I was gazing at the [groups] in Ebor Terrace my eye rested on the long-desired form I immediately quitted the house where I was watched what way you took followed you hither. And now Miss Hart will you be my wife or not, say yes & you make a fellow creature happy for life, say no & you pronounce the death-doom of one who never wronged you" After such an appeal who could have uttered the cold & chilling negation? Lilly could not, she saw at her feet the Grave, the Philosophical Mr Seymour, he who seemed to have subdued all the turbulent passions which agitate other men she beheld him changed for her sake into a mere mortal lover, she heard him declare that his life's happiness depended on her decision & she murmured a faint & faltering yes. "Bless $_{\wedge}^{you}$ my dearest" exclaimed he with energy while he snatched her hand & pressed it passionately to his lips "Bless you for that little word you are now mine & mine alone & nothing save death shall divide us" after a pause he continued in his usual composed & deliberate manner "Circumstances Miss Hart [illegible] which I cannot now explain to you render it imperative that our union should be strictly private, do you agree to this? "I do" she replied for having unconditionally yielded the grand point she could not now hesitate about trifles. "meet me then" proceeded Mr Seymour "To-morrow night at this hour in this place. She consented & after one long & fervent embrace they parted. Some of my readers will doubtless consider that this was an imprudent transaction on the part of Lily but let them remember that she loved Mr Seymour more than her life that besides him there was not one creature on earth in whom she could centre her stock of warm affections & that she was a young & inexperienced girl who had not yet completed her nineteenth year. The whole of the next day Lily employed in making her bridal attire & when it began to grow dark she dressed herself in it. It was a gown of a dark couloured silk such as suited well with her complexion ornamented here & there with small knots of pink ribbon, a larger bow of the same material bound up the rich jetty tresses which otherwise would have hung lower than her waist & made them form a natural corinet on the top of her head. thus simply arrayed she looked most lovely, excitement had restored the bright rose to her cheek & the lustrous light to her eye. And when wrapped in her dark mantle she again passed over Ebor terrace, $^{there\ was\ none}$ amongst all the hundreds there whose tread was so bounding & elastic as her own. The crescent moon was again rising when she entered St Michaels cemetry a gusty Hollow-toned wind waved the great arms of the cypress trees as they stood like swart Giants rising darkly against the twilight sky & the last swell of the vesper organ was dying in the domed

cathedral. Solemn & mournful were the sights & sounds of that darkling hour but her buoyant
spirits resisted the gloomy impression they were calculated to make & full of happy anticipations
she sought her mother's tomb. her heart bounded as she saw a tall figure standing beside it but
in drawing nearer she perceived that it was not her lover but a millitary officer dressed in uniform
his sword & steel clasped belt sparkled in the moonlight & as he paced slowly to & fro with
measured step he hummed the fragment of a merry march. Filled with dismay she was a-
bout to retreat when he suddenly raised his head & exclaimed "Is that you Miss Hart". In the pronunciation of these words, Lily instantly recognized the deep melody of Colonel Percival's [illegible]
peculiarly fascinating voice & the stranger's face being now turned to the light she likewise knew
the statue-like & noble beauty of his features. Now Lily had always admired the Colonel because he was a
handsome & graceful man but she feared him likewise on account of a certain lofty imperiousness in
his manner & in the expression of his bright & bold, dark eyes. His behaviour to her mother & herself had
ever been perfectly kind & gentle, but there was a certain air of condescension mixed with it which
whenever she conversed with him used to impress her with an indescribable feeling of awe. It was there
fore with considerable misgiving & in a very timid tone that she answered [illegible] his question in the affirmative. "Do not be afraid fair Lily" said he encouragingly "I am here on behalf of my friend Mr Seymour
who was prevented from coming himself ^to meet you by urgent business any neglect of which would have excited inquiry & perhaps discovery in which case the happiness he has so much at heart would infallibly have
been snatched away from him at the moment of its completion. I hope you will not refuse to allow me
to act as his substitute" Lily had gone too far to retreat & she was therefore reluctantly compelled to accept of the gay young officer as a conductor. When she had signified that she was ready to follow him he
uttered a shrill whistle & immediately a splendid carriage dashed through the open gates of the cemetry. having assisted her to enter it & placed himself by her side he gave the word of departure & off
they rolled with the ^[celerity] ~~rapidity~~ of lightening. The carriage blinds being down Lily could not discern
which way they went but after an hour's rapid driving the vehicle suddenly drew up & Colonel Percival informed her that she must now alight. On getting out she saw before her the pillared entrance of a vast
park a footman unfolded the gates & her guide drawing her arm through his proceeded to follow the carriage road till they came in sight of a most extensive & magnificent mansion or rather palace whose white
marble columns & turrets were all gleaming with softest radiance in the tranquil moon-beams. he then
turned crossed an angle of the park & open^ing a small arched door which was formed in a lofty wall by which
this portion of the grounds was bounded they entered a large garden. After threading their way through
long [ill.] ^dark alleys through whose bowery arches scarcely a ray of light found ingress & crossing open parterres were the closed & drooping blossoms & variegated green leaves were all wet & glittering with the
tears of night. they at length reached a small chapel or oratory situated in the midst of a great wilderness
of tall & fragrant flowering shrubs "Now ~~said~~ whispered the Colonel as they passed under the fretted porch & up the
long echoing aisle. "Now fair Lily I have discharged my trust & shall yield you to better hands." "And you have discharged it well" said the voice of Mr Seymour issuing from a neighboring aisle "Adrian I thank you but do
not depart till you have seen the indissoluble knot tied. he consented to remain in order to witness

their union & all three proceeded towards the altar were a clergyman of a remarkably grave & venerable aspect stood ready ~~to unite~~ in gown & cassock. In another quarter of an hour Lily Hart had changed her
name & pledged her faith for life. When the marriage ceremony was over Percival took his friend's
hand, warmly wished him joy bade him farewell & after respectfully saluting the bride departed.
"Now my own dear Lilly" said Mr Seymour turning to his wife "We must leave Verdopolis without delay if you do not already feel too much fatigued" Lily assured him that she ~~did~~ was not at all tired
& leaving the chapel they returned to the park-gate where the carriage still awaited their arrival
all night long their journey continued & at last just about sunrise Mr Seymour lifted one of the carriage
blinds & bade his wife look out. She did so & her eye beheld one of the fairest & most fertile [scenes] [illegible]
imagination can conceive. Emerald-green meadows stretched on every side spotted here & there
with tall, spreading forest trees & watered by a broad & placid river, on whose banks facing the east
& bathed in the rosy light of early ~~morning~~ [day] there appeared a small & elegant villa surrounded by a
lawn & gardens & backed by a grove of tall young elm trees whose branches as they were shaken by
the sweet [illegible] morning wind let fall a shower of dew on the clustering vines & roses which
clung to its roof & sides. "What a ~~sweet~~ lovely place" said Lily "I should like to live there. "Your wish is
granted my love." replied her husband "for that is your destined place of abode. And for three years Lily
dwelt in this peaceful little paradise in the midst of as perfect happiness as it is possible for mortal man
or woman to enjoy. Surrounded by all the elegancies & comforts of life, blessed ere long by a beautiful
& healthy boy, cherished by an affectionate & tender Husband whose mild philosophical manners & calm
deep attachment never lost either their charm or their strength who could be happy if she was not?
Yet there were one or two little circumstance which somewhat disturbed her felicity. In the first
place the mystery of their clandestine marriage ~~yet~~ still remained unsolved. she did not yet properly
know who her husband was she had never seen one member of his family or even heard him mention them. his anxiety to keep her in perfect seclusion was evident, he never once permitted her to
visit Verdopolis & no guest with the exception of Colonel Percival was ever allowed to enter Elm-
Grove Villa. In the second place she was often for weeks together deprived of Mr Seymour's own
society, he seldom upon an aggregate spent more than the fourth part of the year with her the
rest being devoted to important business in the city. It is true the brevity & fewness of his visits
rendered them more delightful, but not withstanding this she could [not] help occasionally expressing a
wish that she ~~could~~ [might] see more of one so justly dear to her. One evening at the commencement
of the fourth year of her marriage, she, her husband & Colonel Percival (whom Lily had learned
[to] regard not only without fear but with feelings of the warmest & purest friendship) were all
assembled in the Villa drawing room. It was a wild & tempestuous night, torrents of rain dashed
incessantly against the windows, a gusty wind swept in fierce but wailing howls through the
crashing elm-grove & every now & then ~~this~~ [its] melancholy voice was mingled with the dull
muttering of distant thunder. This war of elements without the villa however seemed only to
increase the cheerfulness of the party within. Lily seated at her harps was utter[ing] tones melodious
enough one would have thought to have charmed the wildest storm that ever [illegible] rushed

with blast & thunder through the midnight heavens. her husband bent over ^her^ listening in wrapt attention to the sweetness of her voice & harp. Now [illegible] As for Colonel Percival he was busily engaged with his pet little Augustus ~~Percival~~ Seymour, now tossing him in his arms now dancing before his dazzled eyes a glittering watch & chain & then again teaching him how to handle & cock a small pistol which he loaded with powder & discharged once or twice which the bold, spirited child instead of being terrified clapped his hands & chuckled with delight at every explosion. "Colonel" said Lily rising when she had ceased her song & advancing towards him with a smile "You will spoil my child by your too great indulgence already he is getting as [illegible] willful & unmanageable as, as," "As myself" madam you would say interrupted the Colonel laughing "be it so I have no desire to see him otherwise, if he could unite a little of my impetuosity with his father's wisdom he would be perfect you know" She was going to reply in the same half playful half serious strain. When a tremendous peal of thunder burst just over their heads" "The storm increases" observed Mr Seymour "how dreadful must be the situation of those who are exposed to its fury" he had scarcely uttered these words when the sound of approaching carriage wheels followed by a violent ringing of the door bell & a correspondingly vigourous agitation of the knocker ^proclaimed^ [illegible] that there were persons without who suffered even now the pitiless drenching of the tempest. Directly after a servant opened the door & announced that a Gentleman & two ladies had arrived in an open chariot & requested shelter till the storm should pass over. Show them into the dining room" said Mr Seymour. "the fire is gone out in that room sir replied the servant & they are dripping wet." "Well then bring them here, I suppose Adrian (looking towards the Colonel) "they are not persons who know anything of us so it does not much signify." Steps were now heard on the staircase, the door was again flung open & there entered first a tall perpendicular, rigid looking old gentleman of about sixty, with high bald forehead, trimed with a fringe of silver hair aquiline nose & very keen, piercing grey eyes. then a lady who had past the meridian of life but still retained in her benevolent countenance & mild blue eyes the remains of what had once been surpassing loveliness, & lastly a tall slender & beautiful girl, both the ladies were envelloped in large dark velvet mantles lined with costly ermine, these rich garments were wet through & clung round them as if they had been flimsy taffeta. the effect which the appearance of this imposing trio produced upon Percival & Seymour seemed very ~~remarkable~~ unaccountable to Lily. The former sprung up exclaiming with an astonished smile "Lord bless me the day of discovery is come at last, the hour when the secrets of all hearts shall be revealed, but never mind John stand it out boldly like a man Flinch not, lie not but make a clean bosom & take what shall ^come^ thereafter." Mr Seymour did not seem greatly to need this advice, he had stood up & with folded arms & an air of cool determination had taken his station just opposite the door. "What means all this my lord marquis?" asked the old gentleman looking sternly at Colonel Percival "Why do I find you & my son here & who is this woman?"That woman" replied Seymour in a firm but respectful tone "That woman, my royal father ^is^ my dear wife Lily marchioness of Fidena. I crowned her with my coronet three years since & there by her side stands my son & your grandson John Augustus Sneaky" The appearance of a thousand disembodied spirits could not have stricken the royal party with more mute astonishment

133

than did this simple peice of intelligence. At length after gazing at his son silently for some minutes the monarch Alexander [ill.] spoke "Do not think to impose on me thus he said "that presumptuous woman shall return immediately to her native obscurity from which you have so wickedly raised her unless you can produce the fullest proof of your marriage & unless that marriage ⟨was solemnized⟩ by the chief Prelate, for no humbler priest can lawfully wed a prince of the blood "I can bear witness to your majesty" replied Colonel Percival or as we must now call him the marquis of Douro for such he really was. "That about this time three years since "John Prince of Fidena was united to Lily Hart by Gravey the metropolitan archbishop himself before the high altar of the Private Chapel situated in the gardens which surround your [ill.] imperial Palace on the banks of the Niger I standing by & giving away the bride with my own hands" A dark & ominous flush covered Alexander's haughty brow when he heard this pronounced by the unabashed marquis in a tone of the most perfect & easy nonchalance what he would have said or done I know not but just as he was about to speak the queen & her eldest daughter lady Edith (my readers will have already recognized these exalted personages in the two females who accompanied him) flung themselves at his feet & implored him to forgive what could not now be undone & to receive ⟨once more⟩ to his paternal favour the son who till now had [illegible] never offended him. Lily trembling like an aspen leaf & pale as her floral namesake joined her tears to their entreaties. Alexander however remained quite unmoved by their supplications & would probably have given free vent to the indignation which boiled within him had not the marquis of Douro stepped up to him & whispered in a low emphatic tone "monarch of the mountains you may indeed cast this son away but where will you turn to find another who shall be more worthy to inherit your crown & throne? nowhere. therefore royalty must depart from your line & the sceptre pass into the hands of aliens" "You have spoken truth" replied the twelve after a pause "there fore prince John I forgive ⟨you⟩ but take notice it is not from the weakness of compassion but merely because Necessity compels me to it. Had I another son who was yet guiltless of any such daring act of disobedience, I would disown you, your wife & child instantly & forever." Prince John made no answer to this speech of his Royal Father's he only bowed low & raising his kneeling wife said with a pride almost equal to that of Alexander himself "Now my Lily you shall appear in the circles for which nature designed you & if anyone dare breathe a word of scorn against you or yours by heaven that word shall be his last. On monday last the marchioness of Fidena made her first public appearance in Verdopolis at a Grand Ball given on the occasion at Elimbos Palace the residence of ~~her~~ the King her Father-in-law. I saw her & can safely state that Lily Hart the widow's daughter is worthy for grace & beauty to rank with the noblest-born & fairest of Verapolis

November
" 7th—33   Charlotte Brontë

"STANZAS ON THE FATE OF HENRY PERCY"

Text adapted from *The Complete Poems of Charlotte Brontë*, ed.
Clement Shorter, bibliography and notes by C. W. Hatfield
(London: Hodder and Stoughton, 1923), pp. 165–74.

The tropic twilight falls, the deep is still;
   All turmoils of the busy day are past;
From the calm lands no voice sounds deep or shrill;
   No murmur from the world of waters vast,
   Save its own ceaseless sound that breeze or blast
Now chafes not into dull or thundering moan.
   The faintest gleam of eve is o'er it cast;
And, oh! how sweet, how holy is the tone
That swells from each green wave, then trembling dies alone!

There's not a boat upon the darkened billow,
   There's not an oar dips in the moonlight main;
Each islander rests on his happy pillow,
   Each swift canoe has sought its home again;
   And neither ringing shout nor trembling strain
Comes from the shore to break the green sea's rest:
   All earth lies hushed to watch the glorious wane
Of that bright sunset from her burning breast;
To see the light of heaven die dim and soft and blest.

Fair southern islands! they are sweetly sleeping,
   While the stars gather in their heaven above,
While sky-breathed airs the deep dark woods are sweeping
   In gales too low to wake the slumbering dove:
   Almost too faint to bend the palmy grove.
Intenser purple grows that kindling dome,
   And brighter flash those orbs of light and love:
Sweet tropic islands! ye are beauty's home;
Oh! who from your bright shores to colder lands would roam?

Midnight is near: that bark upon the water
   Has furled her sails and set her watch on deck:
She rides at anchor, Neptune's noblest daughter:
   The very waves seem subject to her beck;
   They dare not dash her glory to a wreck!
How the cool foam curls round her mighty bows
   As fair as braided pearls on beauty's neck!
How the wild wave more softly gliding flows
Where that proud ocean-queen far down her shadow throws!

A wondrous stranger! from afar appearing,
   Long has she walked the path that leaves no track;
And her brave crew, a thousand hazards daring,

Still scorned to turn their noble vessel back.
   No heart fell cold, no hand grew faint and slack,
As on with heaven above and waves beneath,
   And round a wild horizon, densely black,
They stretched before the trade-gales' fiery breath;
Looked full of joy to hope, and fearlessly to death!

Now all is tranquil: they have gained their bourne,
   The fair blest island of the stormless sea,—
Those happy shores where man may cease to mourn,
   Where all is peace and bliss and harmony;
   Gardens of many a wondrous flower and tree;
Homes of strange birds with wings of rainbow light;
   Shapes formed by nature in her fantasie,
Glowing and fresh and fair and Eden-bright;—
But these were now unseen, beneath the veil of night.

And one within that anchored bark is sleeping:
   The youngest, fairest, bravest of her crew.
Oh! how the stars his brow with light are steeping,
   The sails to his lone berth they tremble through.
   He sleeps on deck, and many a pearl of dew
Gleams in his light hair as unroofed he lies,
   And from the abyss of pure deep speckless blue
A sweet gale round him wildly sings and sighs;
A dirge comes to the ear, so sad each cadence dies.

Would he might waken! some sad dream is on him;
   How heavily the breath flows from his breast!
Some unseen influence strangely dwells upon him,
   Some mournful memory will not let him rest.
   Whate'er it was he calms: the unwelcome guest
Has passed away with all its mystery;
   And now, his clasped hands to his bosom pressed,
He turns his fair face to the solemn sky,
His forehead woos again the low breeze wandering by.

Yes! he has dreamed of one now far away,
   His own sweet Florence,[1] she who was his bride
Ere thirteen summer suns had flung their ray
   With gentlest glow on her youth's springing pride.
   Oh! often had he wandered by her side
Through woodland walks and alleys dimly bright,
   Too happy to discern how fast the tide
Of time was lapsing into shadowy night,
How swift the gloaming veiled each parting ray of light.

And now he saw her in a lofty chamber
   Solemn and grandly vast; he knew it well;
And as a light stole down from lamps of amber
   The veil of years and distance sundered fell.

---

1. Florence Marian Hume (usually called Marian).

Faintly there tolled her father's castle-bell:
It spoke the midnight hour; then all was hushed:
   Round on the panels pictured visions swell
Where forms of buried beauty voiceless blushed,
And the rich silent light more softly o'er them gushed.

Calm, tenderly, and pure the moon was shining;
   Through one vast window its white lustre streamed;
On her it fell, her loveliness refining
   To beauty such as mortal never dreamed.
   Her blue eyes looked to heaven: how bright they beamed!
How their deep zones caught glory from the sky!
   And as the long fringe trembling o'er them gleamed
Their lucid light was almost mystery:
They shone like mirrored stars that glassed in dark waves lie!

Henry! she looks to heaven through that vast sea,
   That boundless ocean decked with isles of light:
Are her thoughts travelling to their home in thee?
   Wake they remembered from the radiance bright
   That fills her eye? A touch of love's own might
Has surely clothed her in such living grace;
   'Tis not the calm serenity of night
That brings the blood so swiftly to her face
Like the clear flush of wine seen through a crystal vase.

Yes, it is love, but not such love as thine:
   Not that pure, young affection of the breast
That used to breathe of peace and bliss divine,
   And o'er her white brow fling a shade of rest.
   Oft with his hand in hers in transport pressed
Henry has watched that calm fall on her cheek,
   And while his own heart felt most deeply blest
Has wished a blush of bashfulness to break:
What seemed to him too still, too sisterly, too meek.

She's not alone—there's one beside her bending:
   Is it a friend? The form is dark and high,—
A magic to the solemn chamber lending.
   Flashes through darkness that refulgent eye—
   Its fixed gaze calls that blush and wakes that sigh,
And well might timid maiden shrink and quail,
   For never yet a shape on earth passed by
So like a spirit in a mortal veil:
The cheek that glows for it will soon turn deadly pale.

At once the chamber fades in slow decay,
   The lights are quenched that erst so softly shone,
The dream revolves, the vast hall melts away,
   And gleaming arch and golden lamp are gone,
   And all is dim and imageless and lone.
But trees are rustling in the darkened air,

And mossy grass the pavement springs upon,
And for the vanished taper's dazzling glare
There dawns a gentle gleam—faint, mellow, mildly fair.

Now o'er the scene a mighty wood is sweeping,
　And long deep glades on through it glimmering go;
Rays of the moon the spectral boughs are steeping:
　They wave in winds whose voice sounds wild and low;
　And from far off a river's dreary flow
Swells ceaseless, though the gale at times be still;
　And though the strange sighs, wandering to and fro
Like spirit's wailings, cease the heart to thrill,
Yet the swift waves rush on of that unpausing rill.

The maiden and the shape stand in the lustre
　Flung from the sky on that star-silvered glade;
Those mighty arching trees that round them cluster
　The flood of glory with their shadows braid;
　And when a sudden wind among them played
They swung like giant phantoms on the grass:
　All their boughs trembled, all their foliage swayed.
Ghosts, such as they, in cloudy gloom might pass
Amid the gleaming pomp of some dread wizard's glass!

The maiden weeps: clear moonlit tears are sparkling
　Upon her cheeks; fast from her eyes they gush.
She looks to *him*: his brow grows strangely darkling;
　His cheek is shadowed with a sudden flush
　Of earnest, eager triumph: that rich blush
Fades not before her mute and sad appeal.
　Now passion's waves of conflict o'er her rush:
The sob, the tear, the pallid brow reveal
How wildly strong the love her heart and spirit feel.

Oh! Henry knows his Florence loves *him* not;
　Not as he would be loved, not as his bride;
Then youthful tenderness is all forgot,
　All vanished in the rapid burning tide
　That flows resistless from those eyes of pride
Flashing into her heart so fixedly.
　The voice of that strange vision by her side
Brings with its sweet, deep music other joy
Than that which erewhile woke to bless her fair-haired boy.

The token of their love is on her finger:
　A golden circlet like a ring of light;
And round her small, sweet lip there seems to linger
　Some saddening touch of memory's holy might.
　The tears, too, glancing as the lamps of night
From their clear sources are not tears of bliss;
　But almost ere they tremble into sight
Her stately lover dries them with a kiss,
And soothes her spirit's awe with some proud warm caress.

Sudden a voice comes to the dreamer's ear
  Mournful and sadly murmured, low and dread:
At first it wailed far off, then whispered near:
  Percy! thy Marian deems her bridegroom dead;
  Lover she mourns not: when the rumour spread
She strove to quench the joy that filled her breast.
  Yes! when she heard that the unfathomed bed
Of the wild sea was by her Henry pressed
She wept that she should feel so deeply, truly blest!

And, Percy! she shall be thy rival's bride;
  She from his hands shall take the marriage wreath,
And, standing at the altar, side by side,
  Each unto each resolves of faith shall breathe—
  Oaths of eternal fealty till death;
And hill and plain shall with that bridal ring;
  Breezes shall waft it with their balmiest breath;
Minstrels shall raise the song and strike the string;
And wide the fires of joy like beacon-lights shall spring.

Full glad shall be her life, in bright halls dwelling
  Beneath the awful light of those loved eyes,
The fount of perfect bliss for ever swelling,—
  Deep, fathomless, exhaustless in the skies,—
  Shall, sparkling to her very lips, arise.
Yet there are warnings of an early end:
  There breathes afar a dreary sound of sighs,
And cold the tears of lonely woe descend:
Shades of untimely death, how silently ye blend!

Percy! thy love so strong, so unreturned,
  Shall be avenged on earth: her time is brief;
The radiant form for whom her spirit burned
  Shall smile awhile, then leave her bowed with grief.
  The reaper's sickle shall cut down the sheaf
While the young corn is budding fresh and green;
  She shall be gathered like a springing leaf;
One year, and that fair plant is no more seen;
Few e'en shall know where once its sunny place has been.

  And never from that vision woke
    The journeyer of the deep:
  Ere the pale light of morning broke
    He slept his final sleep.

  The coral banks of those far isles
    Now pillow Percy's head;
  Their blessed moon for ever smiles
    Above his lonely bed.

  And many a spicy zephyr sings
    Sweet from those radiant skies;

And many a bright bird waves its wings
    Around where Henry lies.

No more his rayless eyeballs shine,
    No more his curls are fair;
For tangled seaweeds wet with brine
    Are garlanding his hair.

But how he died no tongue can tell:
    No eye was there to see;
Yet the winds that were his requiem knell
    They moaned him mournfully.

Some say the decks were red with blood
    And wet with trampling feet;
It recks not: he sleeps in the secret flood
    With surge for his winding-sheet.

APPENDIX II

Excerpts from "Letters from an Englishman" by Patrick Branwell Brontë

Written between 1830 and 1832, this series of imaginary letters from a London banker visiting the Glass Town develops a major segment of the joint epic and makes use of a number of Charlotte's most important characters, including the Marquis of Douro, his brother Lord Charles, John of Fidena, and Alexander Rogue, later Alexander Percy. Much of the narrative concerns the Great Rebellion headed by Rogue: the banker is early taken captive by Rogue, along with Douro and Lord Charles, and the account culminates in the great Battle of Fidena, when Rogue is defeated by Prince John and the captives are rescued.

Text from *The Miscellaneous and Unpublished Writings of Charlotte and Patrick Branwell Brontë*, eds. T. J. Wise and J. A. Symington (London, 1936–1938), 8:114–17, 139, 156–58.

LETTERS FROM: AN ENGLISHMAN
BY Captain Flower F L S S &c
P B Bronte June. 9 1831

LETTER 5

Great glass town

On our entering again the great Glass town on March 15[1] 1831, a scene presented itself which a common observer would perhaps feel disappointed to witness here. To my mind it conveyed more fully than ever the horrors and gloom of an approaching revolution. The din of the factories was silent, the shops were shut up, the theatres closed, the markets empty—not a single woman or child to be seen in the streets, no apparent bustle was seen anywhere, but the persons whom I saw walked along silently with slow steps and thoughtful countenance. This was the scene in the public streets—in the alleys and pothouses it was quite different; here you beheld knots of 300 or 400 of poachers and 'rare lads'

---

1. Last letter dated March 18. This letter also dated at the end March 18.

gathered together reading the newspapers and conversing with an animated voice on the proceedings of the government, but no arms, no manifestations of violence appeared, if we except at the barracks where throngs of armed soldiers were stationed and at the Iron Forge and gun shops which were all at work and crowded with customers. Our chariot drew up at the Marquis's residence, where were Col. Grenville and lord Lofty waiting for him to accompany them to the house of Representatives which was just about to sit. He accordingly, in a short time, drove off thither, accompanied by these two friends and myself. I stationed myself in the gallery to observe the proceeding which promised to be highly animating and important.

Crashey's speech having been read and the accounts of expenditure made, Alexander [Rogue] rose amid cries of 'down with the demagogue'—he said:

'Several of the members of this misnamed honourable house (order) have accused me of turbulence and sedition, but I here declare that I have never been so turbulent as they now show themselves to be—who (putting on a fierce look) who, I ask, accuses me of being a demagogue? Bring him forth and let him prove it if he can. Is to be injured, despised, ruined, thwarted by the Government, to be an outcast from society, to appeal for redress and to have that appeal refused, is this to be a demagogue? If you can prove it I confess myself to be one, (cheers and hisses) but gentlemen your excessive decorum and your ungentlemanly behaviour have quite driven me out of my course. I had risen to offer a reply to Crashey's speech. These are not days for mincing the matter, therefore I will throw off the mask of Flattery and show myself in the simple clothing of Truth, I say gentlemen that this speech will do more to agitate the minds of men than any speech that I have ever made, (increased uproar and cries of 'Turn him out,' 'Order,' &c.) yes, (with a furious look) yes, you do indeed require to be called to order, and if you do not order yourselves, I know who both can and will (here several members got on their legs to answer Rogue, but he with his loud and furious tone drowned their voices so that only he was heard—he went on) I will proceed in spite of you. Crashey begins his speech by saying that he believes us on the verge of a Revolution, that in this city there is a fierce and enterprising populace whose interests lie opposite those of their rulers, and that they are led on by a demagogue whom he will not name—will not name, no, he cannot name him. (Here the confusion rose to an alarming height, several members drew their swords and others, taking their hats, departed saying they would hear no more such wickedness. Silence having been in some measure restored, Rogue went on). He knows not of whom he speaks, but we need not wonder at that for every man must some day fall into dotage.'

Here Col. Grenville, the chairman, rising, said 'This language shall not here be permitted with impunity, officers take this man out and shut the doors.'

Three officers immediately laid hold of Rogue, who resisted not, and conveyed him out of the house. The doors being again shut, the chairman moved that a committee should be formed to enquire into the conduct of Rogue. This was immediately done, and the committee, consisting of Marquis Douro, John Sneaky, Arthur Parry, Captain Flower and 6 others retired after and in a short time returned saying that they thought him no longer fit to sit in that house. He was accordingly expelled by a large majority. The house then separated. Thus ended this stormy debate, a debate which will, I think, end in some tremendous convulsion before to-morrow night.

March 16. This morning I was in the delightful company of Marquis Douro, John and Wilkin Sneaky, Edward Tut Ross and Arthur Parry, 5 of the gayest, most agreeable and most rational young men I have ever seen. Marquis Douro seemed the most learned, John Sneaky the coolest, Wilkin Sneaky the gayest, Tut Ross the most open, and Arthur Parry the most daring. They had all, being military men, come to town for the purpose of gaining glory in the approaching revolution, their declared ambition at present, and they did not care who knew it. I said ambition may be sometimes a laudable motive. Upon the ruling motive of their minds Arthur Parry starting up said, 'Sir it is always a laudable motive. The world has long been in the dark about it. Was man formed to lie idle and inactive?' To this they all cried 'No, you say right Arthur.' But while we were thus talking the loud report of a cannon followed by a sharp fire of musketry made us all start up. 'Whatever is that?' said Wilkin. 'Let us see what it is,' answered the Marquis, and immediately they all grasped their swords, put on their military caps and rushed with one accord into the street, and a fine appearance they made as they darted along with the speed of 5 young greyhounds. As soon as they were gone I ascended a tower of one of the cathedrals to obtain a view of what was doing [Here there is a small pen-and-ink portrait] in the city, and there I saw a dense mass of armed men blocking up the whole of St. George's Street. Their number could not be less than 300,000. These men were engaged in a desperate conflict with the military who were, with sabres and bayonets, trying to disperse them but with no avail. After great hesitation a tremendous fire was opened upon them from the castle battery which overlooked the street. This mowed down thousands at once shaking the houses and breaking the windows of the whole quarter of the city. Volley after volley followed so quickly and with such effect that the immense mob first began to stagger, and at length fled in good earnest, pursued by a body of 3000 Lancers who, charging on while they were flying, so completed their overthrow that in half an hour not a man of them was to be seen. When the dreadful affair was over, I descended from my eminence into the street where the battle had taken place. Here the heaps of dead and wounded were lying piled up in masses 4 or 5 feet high, while at every turn I observed persons washing out the blood from their houses into which streams of it had run through the spaces under the doors. The stones of the pavement were all broken and shattered in pieces and the streets were all ploughed and absolutely ripped up by the cannon-balls.

*   *   *

The LETTER X.

Fidena
March 11.

That shout of which I spoke in my last letter was not, as all expected, the signal that Rogue had commenced the storming of Fidena, but proceeded from a very different cause. It appears that Sneaky's Government, having awoke to a sense of their danger, had roused and ordered forth an army under the command of John Sneaky, to march after, attack and destroy the army of the Rebels. This Force after many forced marches, had come in sight just as Rogue with his 3000 men were rushing forward to charge the gates of Fidena. Sneaky's horse to the number of 7000 men instantly galloped in between Rogue at Fidena and us on the hill thus in a masterly manner separating the two parts of our army. This happened just as night was coming on and therefore we knew nothing of the state of our commander, but were in a dreadful state of suspense and anxiety. This was not, however, the case with the Marquis, Young Soult and myself, whose only hope lay in defeat of the rebels. . . .

LETTER XIV

. . . not a moment had elapsed when, bloody with spurring, fiery hot with haste, shouting and tearing up the ground beneath their feet, a vast body of cavalry headed by Sneaky himself rushed into the square and commenced hacking and hewing with their sabres on every side. At this moment I beheld a number of men dragging along the Marquis of Douro, Young Soult, and Charlie, all bound and bloody. As they went by they seized me,

142

tied me, and hurried us all into the thickest of the conflict. There they placed us together. Rogue at this moment rode up and said, 'now you wretches I'll punish you. I could not before but you've got it now.' He then departed. The Marquis said nothing but 'Fiend' and stood motionless, his eyes flashing fire and his face as pale as death. The crush and hurry around us was terrible. Lances and bayonets were constantly darting round us, multitudes were falling like hail at our feet. In a short time a ball struck Young Soult. He sunk on his knees, gave a groan and fell. A shower of dead and dying hid him immediately from our eyes. Directly after, a ball hit Charles—he cried out 'Arthur save me' clung to his brother for a moment but was soon knocked off by a dead body falling on him, and lay motionless. I shall never forget the expression of Arthur's countenance at this moment. His eyes strained as if they would burst, and blazed with a maniacal lustre. The sweat started to his cold forehead, he clenched his teeth and muttered, 'Yes, I will save you.' With one mighty effort he broke his bands like packthreads, seized the first sword he found with an energy that made the blood spring out at his finger nails, and threw himself on the thickest of Rogue's troops. He whirled his sword round with force of resistless lightening, at every blow some man dropped. He espied Rogue at a little distance. I saw him dart forward, spring against his horse with such a force as to throw him on his knees and, lifting his sword, whirl it and himself full in front of the demagogue. All three fell at once together. I saw no more, for a ball at this moment struck me, a mist came across my sight and I fell. It was again my fortune to recover from this shot. When I recovered from this swoon, I found myself in bed in a large lighted room. I, for a moment, thought all that I had witnessed was a dream, but the bandages and plasters round my head soon convinced me to the contrary. In beds opposite to me were laid Young Soult and Charlie, both still senseless, for they moved not. I sat up in bed and undrew the curtain of the window and looked out. The night was cold and rainy. Before me lay a vast yard surrounded by high gloomy houses, partly unroofed and shattered with balls. This vast yard or square was filled with human beings. In the middle was an empty space floored with black cloth and the paling round it covered with the same. Dead silence and utter motionlessness pervaded the vast assemblage below me till a swaying to and fro among them announced the approach of some one. It was the Kings, Sneaky, Wellington, Parry and Stumps, who with their attendants ranged themselves on one side of the open space. Next followed 10 soldiers with muskets guarding a tall man dressed in black, with a countenance as pale as death. I fell back on the bed breathless, for it was Alexander Rogue. When I looked again he was standing erect at one end of the area with a white handkerchief in his hand. The soldiers were ranged opposite about 12 paces distance with their pieces levelled. All was silence, you might indeed have heard a pin drop. At length Rogue called out in a firm clear but sepulchral tone 'Gentlemen FIRE.' My head grew dizzy. The soldiers fired. I saw a bright flash and a loud crash. He fell dead.

Alexander ROGUE

was no more.

P.S. Before morning Y Soult and Charlie awoke from their swoon and the surgeons entering pronounced none of us three dangerously hurt. Afterwards the Marquis entered. He looked dreadfully exhausted from efforts of the night before, for this night was not the night of the battle but the one after. He stated that when he attacked Rogue his sabre broke through his helmet and stunned him, so he immediately seized him and dragged him to the Kings. I knew the rest. Good night. I myself am dreadfully exhausted and can write no more.

Ever yours
J Bellingham

P B Brontë August 2. A.D. 1832.

Two Tales by Charlotte Brontë: "The Secret" & "Lily Hart"
Transcriptions and commentary by William Holtz
Designer, Edward King; house editor, Susan E. Kelpe
Composed in Monotype Dante, a face designed by Giovanni
Mardersteig, by William Clowes & Sons, Ltd., London
Printed offset on one-hundred-pound white Mohawk Super-
fine High Finish by Meriden Gravure, Meriden, Connecticut
Bound in Göppinger Iris 101 with leather spine, with eighty-
pound Strathmore Deep Blue Pastelle Text endpapers, by
Robert Burlen & Son, Inc., Hingham, Massachusetts